CAGED

GOLD HOCKEY #11

ELISE FABER

CAGED
BY ELISE FABER
Newsletter sign-up

CAGED
Copyright © 2021 Elise Faber
Print ISBN-13: 978-1-63749-002-0
Ebook ISBN-13: 978-1-63749-001-3
Cover Art by Jena Brignola

GOLD HOCKEY SERIES

***Gold Hockey* (all stand alone)**
Blocked
Backhand
Boarding
Benched
Breakaway
Breakout
Checked
Coasting
Centered
Charging
Caged
Crashed
A Gold Christmas
Cycled
Caught
Cap

GOLD CAST OF CHARACTERS

Heroes and Heroines:

Brit Plantain (Blocked) — first female goalie in the NHL, loves boy bands

Stefan Barie (Blocked) — captain of the Gold

Sara Jetty (Backhand) — artist and figure skater

Mike Stewart (Backhand) —defenseman for the Gold, romance guru

Blane Hart (Boarding) — center for the Gold, number 22

Mandy Shallows (Boarding) — trainer and physical therapist

Max Montgomery (Benched) — defensemen for the Gold, giant nerd

Angelica Shallows (Benched) — engineer at RoboTech, also a giant nerd

Blue Anderson (Breakaway) — top forward in the league and for the Gold

Anna Hayes (Breakaway) — Max's former nanny, no relation to Kevin Hayes

Rebecca Stravokraus (Breakout) — Gold publicist, makes killer brownies, known at PR-Rebecca

Kevin Hayes (Breakout) — forward for the Gold, no relation to Anna Hayes

Rebecca Hallbright (Checked) — nutritionist for the Gold, plethora of delicious vegan recipes, known as Nutrionist-Rebecca

Gabe Carter (Checked) — doctor, head trainer for the Gold

Calle Stevens (Coasting) — assistant coach for the Gold, former national team member

Coop Armstrong (Coasting) — talented forward on the Gold, addicted to historical romance audiobooks

Mia Caldwell (Centered) — 5th degree black belt, brings the snark

Liam Williamson (Centered) — Gold forward finding his love for the game, charming and pushy in equal measures

Charlotte Harris (Charging) — new Gold GM, hates losing and the game Chubby Bunny

Logan Walker (Charging) — defensemen for the Gold, skills include: cockiness and being able to buy presents that make Charlotte squirm

Dani Eastbrook (Caged) — video coach for the Gold, tech nerd, could fix your computer in a flash, shy

Ethan Korhonen (Caged) — forward for the Gold, killer power play skills, known as Big Juicy Brain

Devon Scott (Block & Tackle) — former player, current owner Prestige Media group

Becca Scott (Block & Tackle) — Devon's assistant

Additional Characters:

Fanny — skating coach

Bernard — head coach

Richie — equipment manager

Dan Plantain — Brit's brother

Diane Barie — Stefan's mom

Pierre Barie — Stefan's dad, owner of the Gold

Spence — former goalie, married to Monique, daughter Mirabel

Monique — married to Spence, former model

Mirabel — daughter of Spence and Monique
Mitch — Sara's boss
Allison and Sean — Blane's parents
Pascal — Devon Scott's security lead
Roger Shallows — Mandy's dad
Grant and Megan — Devon's parents

ONE

DANI

S hy.

She was painfully shy.

Great with tech. Horrible with people.

But that was okay because her job *was* tech. As a video coach for the Gold, her livelihood depended on how well she could interact with the tech surrounding her at any given time—tech that currently consisted of multiple monitors on her office wall, a desktop, a laptop, and a trio of tablets. She actually had a dozen tablets at her disposal, but the rest were currently being used by the coaching staff.

The Gold had just finished their third game of the season, and though she wouldn't say her job got lighter as the season progressed, this time, in particular, was dizzying.

There were new players to get up to speed.

Changes to the system that needed to be addressed.

Specific plays the coaches wanted highlighted.

And she was down her assistant—who was out with the stomach flu—and an intern—who'd lied on his resumé, couldn't actually isolate and/or edit video, and hated everything to do with the game of hockey.

Video. Coach.

Both of those were important—okay, both were *critical* to her job.

She needed to understand the game, needed to be able to anticipate what the players and coaching staff would need, *and* she needed to be able to move fast to isolate, tag, and make that content available, both during and after each of the eighty-two regular-season games, not to mention any additional playoff games the team might be lucky enough to participate in.

So, an intern with no interest in the sport was useless.

And an assistant coach, who was confined at home with the stomach plague, was similarly not helpful for the fingertip tap dance she had to conduct during a normal game. It meant she'd played double-duty for the contest, watching eight feeds at once, layering alternate angles together of different parts of the matchup —zone entries, injuries, penalties, or power plays—in addition to being prepared to advise the bench coaches on whether or not to challenge a particular goal.

In a word, by the time she was finishing up her end of the game process—superimposing stats pulled by the NHL onto the various video clips and making them accessible to players and coaches alike—Dani was exhausted.

But, crying over spilled milk and all that.

She didn't have time for exhaustion or crying or . . . well, not much except to be staring lovingly into her screens, her fingers caressing the keyboards and tablets . . . and yes, she realized that her referring to staring lovingly and caressing anything tech-related meant that she'd probably been single far too long.

Not that single was an uncommon adjective to describe Dani Eastbrooke.

It was usually included, right along with quiet, shy, and painfully awkward.

"Stop," she whispered. She was who she was, and she didn't

have time for reminiscing or self-flagellation, not when she had enough work for three people and only one person to do it.

A ping came across her cell.

Glancing down, she saw it was a request—or technically, *three* more requests, and . . . see? No time to think about her pathetically empty life.

On that pleasant thought, she straightened her shoulders and rolled out her neck, focusing on the screen in front of her as she began transferring the video.

Then turned and focused on the next one, repeating the process.

Once the third was complete, she gathered the tablets, pushed out of her chair, and hurried into the hall.

"Oof!" She skidded to a stop, warm hands gripping her shoulders, steadying her.

Unfortunately, she'd hurried without looking.

Unfortunately, because the tablets she'd been holding tumbled from her grip, hitting the ground with a sickening *crunch.* Yes, they had protective covers. No, she didn't normally launch them at concrete floors.

Also *unfortunately,* because she had crashed into a giant muscled mass of sweaty man. He was tall and blond and too fucking pretty for her mental well-being, especially with gentle gray eyes sliding to hers, with the warmth of his large hands soaking through the fabric of her shirt.

A sliver of heat slid through her stomach.

Oh, *no.*

That would not do.

Tearing her eyes away, she dropped to her knees and picked up the first tablet she could reach, running her finger over the screen and checking for damage.

"Do you stroke everything so carefully?"

Desire coated her spine in honey, filled her throat with cotton.

She glanced up, saw that he'd crouched next to her, and in an instant, was lost again in his eyes, the pale gray of the sky hinting at a thunderstorm.

Storm.

Well, *that* was fitting, considering the storm that had awakened inside her the first time she'd seen this man. God, she could still remember how every cell in her body had stood up and taken notice, and that had just been the result of viewing him through her monitor, just after he'd joined the team. Tall and big and yet somehow still graceful, even despite the beard and the tattoo peeking out of the collar of his jersey. From the first moment she'd laid eyes on Ethan, he'd reminded her of a giant grizzly bear, something any smart human had to fight the urge to not cuddle with.

Fluffy, but would tear a woman to shreds with those razor-sharp claws.

"Dani?"

"No," she said simply and reached for the next tablet, doing a visual scan this time instead of any *stroking*. When it looked okay, she thrust it at him, at Ethan Rogers, at the sexiest man she'd ever laid eyes on. "Here. This is the one Calle wanted you to have."

"No stroking?" he said, almost lazily, taking the tablet from her with a slow brush of his fingers against hers.

More heat—sparking up her arms, sliding down her torso, pooling in her stomach.

Her words stoppered up in the back of her throat.

She simply shook her head in response.

"Dani?" he asked; the heat tempered, curiosity in its place. He was still crouching next to her, the smell of spice and male filling the air. Probably, the strong scent should have been off-putting. Instead, it was tempting, drawing her in like catnip, but she couldn't look up at him, not even when he stayed still, stayed near, clearly waiting for her to speak or meet his gaze.

One rough finger brushed the back of her hand.

Sparks.

Gasping, her eyes flew up, collided with his gaze. Her heart absolutely pounded, but other than that single touch, he didn't make any other moves to close the distance between them.

"Dani?" he asked again.

"Yeah?" she whispered.

"Why don't you like me?"

Her jaw dropped open. Why didn't *she* like *him*? Dani drooled after Ethan on a regular basis. She had dreams about him, had named her favorite vibrator after him.

See? Good with tech.

With people—including the gorgeous man all of two feet away? Horrible.

But what *could* she say? It wasn't like she was going to share the name of her vibrator. Hell, she might as well be honest, she wasn't going to share *anything*. This is what she did.

She got shy. She got quiet. She came off as a royal bitch.

"Y-you're fine," she finally managed, reaching for the last tablet, intending to find a way to bolt, to end her misery, and GTFO.

But he stood when she did, those gray irises dancing with mirth. "Fine?"

"I—uh—" Her cheeks burned, and worse, she felt tears prickle at the backs of her eyes.

Ugh. She hated that she did this, too.

Pushing past him, she tried to bolt.

"Hey," he said, catching her arm. "*Hey,*" he said again, releasing her when she yanked fiercely at his grip. "I'm just teasing."

She shrugged, stepped away, cheeks hot, eyes still stinging, her throat tight, her lips and mouth and tongue barely able to form words. "Right," she managed after a painfully long time.

"Dani?" Another gentle question, and God, she liked the way he said her name, soft with a bit of a rasp, more grizzly vibes, more urges to cuddle.

Her shoulders tensed.

A soft chuckle.

Ethan was close enough that she would swear she could feel that small laugh skate over her skin. "I actually came to find you."

She gaped, heart pounding.

He'd come to find *her?* That just didn't compute.

"Me?"

He nodded.

She lost her words again. Because seriously, what universe was she currently living in?

"I wanted to ask you a question—"

Ah.

Her heart skittered to a stop, resignation sailing through her as she realized what was going down. This was how all of these types of conversations began. People like Ethan sought her out, not because they wanted to have a conversation or hang, but because they needed help with their TV or laptop or cell phone.

Ethan, she guessed, would need laptop help.

He looked like he could handle a cell or a television.

And no, don't ask her how she knew what he needed help with, okay?

She'd been through this rodeo many a time before. Dani's tech guru-ness was a gift that had been bestowed upon her at birth . . . okay, *fine,* it had been honed by many lonely preteen and teenage years.

"I can fix your computer," she said, trying to pretend that she wasn't miserable at the prospect, that she didn't want someone to come to her for once for some other reason.

It was a *good* thing they didn't. Really. It was.

She wouldn't know what to do with them if they did.

Except, over the last few months, she had to wonder if she was selling herself short, if perhaps she'd sat back on her shy laurels for too long, used them as an excuse to keep people at a distance.

A snort bubbled up in her throat.

Or course she did.

That was her M.O. Always had been, always would be.

"What?" Ethan asked. "My computer isn't . . ." He trailed off, and with her brows drawing together, she considered if perhaps her guru skills were out of practice. She hadn't been hit up *too* often since she'd joined the Gold.

"Then you need help with your phone?" she asked.

He frowned, shook his head. "No."

She tilted her head to the side, curiosity overshadowing her shyness for a moment, feeling herself intractably pulled into those gray eyes. "Your TV?"

"No, Dani," he said on a husky laugh, and she ignored the prickles of desire trailing over her skin.

"Oh." She swallowed. "Okay then." She turned away.

"Are you seeing anyone?"

Slowly, she spun back, eyes wide.

"That was my question," he said, when she stared at him in shock. "Dani?" he asked, when she just continued staring at him mutely. "Did I break you?"

A slow shake of her head.

He stepped a little closer, just near enough that she could feel the heat from his body. "No to the breaking you part, or no to the seeing anyone piece?" he murmured.

"The seeing anyone thing," she somehow managed to whisper, despite the fact that the question from a man like him to a woman like her was absolutely one hundred percent unfathomable.

Circling back to sad and single and—

He smiled.

And she actually felt her brain cells collide and fizzle into smoke. That smile was dangerous, could without a doubt, turn her stupid. *Really* stupid.

"Good," he murmured.

Swallowing hard, she nodded, cheeks on fire, and turned away again. "Right, I'll just—"

"Will you go out with me?"

Her fingers went limp. The tablets hit the ground. This time, the *crunch* sounded much more ominous. Or maybe that was just her heart.

Two

Ethan

He winced when the tablets hit the floor again and bent over to scoop them up.

Shit.

One corner was cracked, but Ethan supposed that wasn't the first nor would it be the last time something like that had happened. Still, he'd offer to pay for it. He didn't like the idea of the team having to eat the cost for something he'd caused.

The other was unscathed.

Dani, however, appeared to be *very* scathed. Her mouth gaped, and he could swear there was pink warming the brown tones of her umber-colored skin, making him wonder what exactly had brought on the blush.

Was it that she was embarrassed he'd asked and felt uncomfortable?

That made a sick pit open up in his stomach.

"I—I—" She shook her head. "I—"

"It's okay," he said quickly, stepping back. "No hard feelings."

Deep brown brows drew down. "H-hard feelings?"

"You're not interested." He took another step back, *all* the hard feelings ruminating through him, but unwilling to let them escape, to taint their workplace. He wanted her, but he wasn't that guy. Wouldn't ever be. "I promise, I won't bring it up again."

Her mouth opened and closed, words stuttering out. "I—I—"

"It's fine," he said quickly. "You want me to bring these to the guys?"

"I—"

Another few feet away. "I'll just—"

"Will you stop interrupting me?" she snapped.

He blinked.

Her chin lifted and for a moment, he was frozen in place by her eyes. They were brown—he'd known that from the glimpses she'd given him before—but what he *hadn't* known was that they weren't *just* brown. Shades of russet and amber, speckles of gold, streaks of ebony. No, those uniquely gorgeous irises couldn't simply be categorized as brown. They were . . . spectacular and entrancing and—

Dani kept talking, drawing him out of his head.

"I'm shy," she said. "But I'm not stupid. I can tell someone when I'm uncomfortable or if I don't want something."

Hope bloomed through him.

"Does that mean you *want* to go out with me?"

Her eyes widened, her mouth opening and closing. "I—um—I—"

This time he didn't interrupt, just waited for her to get her thoughts together, her words to catch up, and all the while the prospect of being able to take out this woman he'd admired for so long lingered in the back of his mind.

"I don't think that's a good idea," she whispered. "I need to get these to Max and Coop."

Bleak.

That was the only word to describe what he felt at the moment. But he'd meant it when he'd promised himself that if she didn't return his interest, he wouldn't press this, that he'd just go back to pretending he wasn't attracted to her.

"Okay," he said, holding up the tablets. "I'll take these to the locker room."

She nodded.

"For the record, I never thought you were stupid," he said, "and I don't mind the shy." With that, he turned and made his way down the hall, cursing himself six ways to Sunday as he moved. He should have played it so much cooler, should have won Dani over before springing a date on her. He should—

"Fuck," he whispered on a sigh.

Because he *had* been trying to win her over these last months, finding reasons to be in her presence—e.g. tonight volunteering to grab tablets she was going to deliver, asking for extra tape, casually joining the conversations when she was with Brit or Mandy, testing the waters when she was with people she was comfortable with.

And he'd thought he'd made progress with trying to get her to talk and loosen up.

So today, tonight, he'd hoped for her to let him in just an inch.

Too fast.

Fucking hell.

Ethan knew that most of the guys on the team thought that Dani was a little cold. But most of the guys were idiots. Okay, *that* wasn't true, not even in the least. The San Francisco Gold were the NHL's newest team—though that would soon change with several more expansion teams entering the mix next season—and they were one of the best franchises to play for. He'd been around for the last win of the Stanley Cup and for last season's heart-breaking loss. Before that, he'd bounced around the league, playing a few seasons with different teams. But nothing had ever stuck. Or maybe, the roster hadn't gelled like the Gold's did.

Or perhaps . . . it was because the Gold were more like a family than a business.

Which should sound ridiculous because it *was* a business, and hockey was his job.

But somehow, it *wasn't* ridiculous.

The men and women on the team were a family. Without qualification. As obvious as a crosscheck to his opponent's numbers would get him sent to the box. It was just . . . fact.

What was also fact?

That even now, well after the game, the locker room would still be full of the guys and Brit shooting the shit, hanging around because they actually liked each other.

A rare feat indeed.

Laughing to himself as he strode through the door, handing the tablets to Max and Coop, he thought back on his first game with the team. God, it had been such a weird feeling, as though he'd ended up in an alternate reality.

There wasn't the least bit of hazing or him needing to earn his spot. They'd included him, given him the benefit of the doubt, and right away, he'd felt like he had a place.

They'd invited him to dinner after the match.

They'd actually included him in the conversation from the get-go—as well as giving him an assigned day on manning the radio. The latter was something everyone took turns with, and though the guys had some overlap in taste, it was something of a rite of passage to get your pregame playlist poked at.

Today's *post*game playlist was Brit's choice, which meant that as he finished getting undressed and headed to the showers, he was serenaded by various boy bands with syrupy lyrics and poppy soundtracks.

The songs were fucking catchy, he'd give Brit that.

But he much preferred his classic rock pre or postgame.

He wondered what kind of music Dani listened to, though he supposed he wouldn't be in a position to find out.

"What's going on in that big, juicy brain of yours?" Max asked, when Ethan sat back down in his stall and began pulling his clothes on.

Big, juicy brain was the team's favorite way to refer to him.

A guy works on getting one master's degree, and suddenly he was everyone's favorite nerd.

But seriously, what else was there to do when a man was on the road for half a season and drinking and partying got really old? Plus, his parents were professors, had always teased each other about being career students. It would have been a surprise if he didn't follow in their footsteps, at least a little bit. "What are you talking about?" he muttered.

"You look all mopey," Max said, bending and tying his shoes.

Ethan scowled but didn't otherwise comment as he yanked on his underwear and slacks, began buttoning his shirt.

"You've got a little frown in between your brows. Angie would say you're being all scowly."

"Did you just do air quotes?"

A shrug. "They're endearing."

"No," Ethan said. "They're really not."

"So, does the mope have to do with a certain brunette who won't give you the time of day?"

Ethan's eyes shot up, a critical error that had him giving away his hand before he'd been ready to. This was why he was shit at poker, and he knew he was fucked when Max's eyes sharpened. He was one of the worst gossips on the team, perhaps only eclipsed by Brit.

Though, Coop was honing his skills.

Pretty soon, they'd have three Musketeers to contend with.

Ethan shoved his shoes on. "I don't know what you're talking about."

"Hmm," Max said, leaning back in his stall and crossing his arms behind his head, "and here I thought you'd be better at lying."

Ethan laughed. "You saw me last poker night. How could you possibly think that?"

Max smirked. "True." A beat. "So, win Dani over yet?"

He froze. Fucking motherfucker was such an asshole . . . and too damned inquisitive for anyone's good. "Don't you have to get home to your family?" he grumbled.

"Not right at the moment."

Great. He sighed, slipped into his jacket, then risked a look out of the corner of his eye.

Max was still staring at him.

"What?" he asked again. "I'm not talking about Dani."

"Ah. No progress. You okay?"

"I'm fine." He shrugged. "It's . . . not fine, but I'm not going to pursue something she doesn't want. I'm not an asshole."

"No, you're not. I'm sorry it didn't work out." His face went serious. "I could—"

"No. Thanks, though, man."

Max nodded, was surprisingly quiet as they went through the remaining motions of getting ready to go.

"So, aside from the lack of progress with the unnamed brunette tech guru, I also detect a dash of sad. Did you fail a pop quiz or something?"

"No, I most certainly did not," he said.

"You're getting straight As, aren't you?"

"My GPA is beside the point." He grinned. "Also, so what if I am?"

Max slugged him. "Brawn. Brains. It's not fair, man. Look at *this*"—he held up his arm, pointed to his bicep, which was respectable in the hockey realm where lean strength was valued over grizzly bear status like Ethan had—"it's puny in comparison."

"You have tree trunks like this," Ethan said, holding up his own arm, "and you'd crush Angie. She's tiny."

"Maybe."

"Speaking of Angie, I heard she was pregnant again. Congrats."

Max smiled. "Thanks, man."

"Is Brayden excited to be a big brother again?" he asked.

"He's a teenager," Max said. "He's not excited about much,

unless it's some new TikTok trend." A sigh. "But he didn't sulk off to his room"—Max smiled—"and he stopped after school today to pick up Angie's favorite milkshake from the Dairy, so really, even though he is a teenager, he isn't *too* bad of one."

"Brayden's a good kid."

Max shook his head, still smiling. "Yeah, he is."

Brit walked up, waved a hand in his direction. "What's going on with this face?"

Ethan sighed, waited for Max to dish.

Surprisingly, he didn't, just silently watched Brit as she studied him with laser focus.

"I failed that pop quiz you were teasing me about earlier," he said.

A blip of quiet, Brit's expression stern. "So, you're not going to tell me why you're scowly and moody?"

No fucking way. But he didn't say that, just lifted a brow and waited.

Silence.

Max stood up, clapped Ethan on the shoulder. "See ya." And then the fucker walked off, leaving him in Brit's clutches.

"Spill," she ordered. "Tell me how I can help."

And *that* right there was why the nosiness was tolerable, even welcome, though significantly less so when it was directed at him. Because Brit and everyone else on this team actually gave a shit. They wanted to know every detail, yes, but it wasn't to ridicule and scorn. It was because they wanted everyone to be happy.

"Want to be my study buddy?"

Brit's eyes narrowed. "Sure, you failed that quiz, Eth." She pointed two fingers at herself then at Ethan. "Watching you."

Max poked his head back into the conversation. "And you know the gossip train is, too." He lifted a fist, raised it up and down. "*Choo-choo!*"

"You guys are hilarious," Ethan muttered.

"Damn right, we are." And with that, Max walked out of the locker room, waving goodbye to the rest of the team, most of whom were in various states of their postgame routine or getting ready to follow him out.

Brit gave him one narrowed look then turned and hit the showers.

Ethan sighed. He still had the video to watch—and wounds to lick— but he could do both of those from the space of his own house.

He'd bring the tablet back tomorrow.

Slipping his wallet into his pocket, the tablet into his backpack, which he then shrugged on, Ethan found himself drawn into a conversation with Blane, and while he liked his teammate, a whole hell of a lot, he really wanted to go home, have a beer—since it was close enough to his cheat day tomorrow that he didn't have to worry about Nutritionist Rebecca giving him a hard time about veering off his specially designed diet plan. He was typically a firm believer in the what-she-didn't-know-didn't-hurt her approach to dealing with nutritionists, but the team had bought into Rebecca's plans long ago and truthfully, even though the diet was a bit restrictive, especially for his meat-loving heart, he'd never felt or played better. So, it hadn't taken him long to get on board.

Especially, when she'd worked in those cheat days *and* he could have a beer and burger every once in a while.

"Eth?"

He turned, saw that Brit was back, staring at him, her long, blond hair slicked back after her shower. "What's up?"

She crossed to him, voice quiet when she said, "You know that play wasn't on you, right?" Her nose wrinkled in a way that was decidedly cute and definitely not in the typical tough hockey player realm—but that was Brit, a constant in juxtapositions.

It didn't take much to understand what play she was referring to, especially because it *was* his fault. He'd misjudged an angle, the player from the other team had gotten by him, and he hadn't made it back in time. They'd scored, and it *had* been on him.

"I mean," she said softly. "Shit happens, and it's on everybody, not just one person."

Still, it was easier to let her think that he was upset about the play instead of his failed wooing techniques with Dani.

"Nice try." He bumped her shoulder with his when she sat beside him. "You know damned well it was my fuck up, but"—here he sighed and told the truth, and conveniently, it applied to both the play and the shit with Dani—"I can't do anything about it, so I'm going to go home, have a couple of hours' early cheat day, and I'm going to wallow in my ineptitude. And then tomorrow," he added quickly, when her expression turned concerned. "I'll be over it, and all will be good."

Her eyes narrowed. "You promise?"

"Yes, Mom," he teased lightly.

"So not funny," she said.

"Why?" he asked.

A roll of her eyes. "Stefan wants a baby. He's 'willing to wait' as long as I want," she said. "But he also said that he wouldn't mind if I didn't take such a long contract next time so that he's not a grandpa by the time we have our first."

He sat back in his stall, brows lifting. Now *this* was interesting.

"I mean," she whispered, "I *want* kids. It's just that I don't know if I want them when I'm away so much, but I'm not ready to stop playing, and getting pregnant would mean . . ."

She kept talking, and he'd been part of the team long enough to find this particular bit of gossip fascinating—especially when she was freely offering it up. Though he supposed she didn't have much to hide after she'd fallen in love with and married the former captain of the team *and* spent the majority of her time poking her nose in other people's business. However, that notwithstanding, Brit was great with kids, even if it was obvious that a woman couldn't be pregnant with men shooting pucks at her a hundred miles per hour, not to mention the collisions she took sometimes.

Kids would have to wait until after she retired.

Unless . . .

"You could always adopt," he said.

Her brows lifted, her lips freezing in the middle of describing what Stefan would look like as a grandpa. "I could adopt?" she mouthed.

He nodded.

"Holy shit," she whispered. "Stefan and I could *adopt*."

Ethan patted her on the shoulder. "You'd both be great parents." He'd met Stefan, who'd retired from the team a few seasons back, enough times over the last couple of years to know the other man fairly well. He was a good guy, treated Brit like the goddess she was, and he'd never seemed to hold her successful career against her, even though he was no longer playing.

In fact, Stefan had a reserved seat at the Gold Mine, directly behind Brit's net.

Not the best position for viewing the game.

But perfect for watching his wife kill it, as she did on most nights.

"I—" she whispered. "You think so?"

"Yes, I do." With that, he patted her shoulder again and decided to take advantage of her befuddlement by calling out his goodbyes and hightailing it out of the locker room.

Babies.

They shouldn't be the obvious conversational topic for big, tough hockey players, but they were common subjects of banter in the Gold's locker room because the kids were folded right into the rest of the team. They were family, too, along with the coaches, with the equipment managers and trainers and support staff. Wives and girlfriends, too. Brothers and sisters, moms and dads.

All were commonly seen.

And the team played the better for it.

It was just . . . today, he was missing that he didn't have more to add to the group. Sure, his parents came to some games, but they were busy, they had their own lives, and those lives didn't revolve around his any longer.

Which was fine.

He was a thirty-year-old man, not a child who needed a ride to early-morning practices and away games.

Not anymore, anyway.

Smiling as he walked to his car thinking of what his mom would say if he called her and teasingly asked her to drive him to the rink, he didn't see the flurry of silken brown hair, the lush, curvy body.

Not until it was too late.

And for the second time in one night, he collided with the woman he'd been dreaming about for months.

THREE

The universe hated her.

That was the only explanation she had for why she was plastered against Ethan's chest for a second time that evening.

He smelled good, all spicy and male, his hair still damp from the shower.

It was funny, though, for as long as his beard was—a bushy gathering on his jaw—his hair was neatly trimmed, as it always was.

"Are you growing it out?" she blurted, still in his arms, her fingers lifting to trace the bristles, finding they were softer than she expected. Also, such an inappropriate thing to do, paired with an unsuitable question for a workplace, where she liked to at least pretend she was professional, even though she spent many of her waking—and sleeping—hours fantasizing about this man. Dani could also add that it was remarkably tactless to be stroking his jaw, since she'd just turned the man down when he'd asked her out.

So, no.

She shouldn't be looking at his beard, let alone commenting on it.

Or thinking how it might feel between her thighs.

His hands had been resting on her shoulders again, the warmth seeping through her team jacket, making her nerves skip and fire with need, but her words had him lifting one, resting it against hers on his jaw and rubbing lightly.

She heard the bristling sound—*no,* she actually felt it, and not just on her palm. The slight rasp skated over her middle, both dipping down and shooting up, her nipples hardening against the fabric of her bra, her legs quivering.

"Not intentionally," he said, voice husky, his gray eyes the color of clouds readying to drop buckets full of rain. "My trimmer broke, and I just got lazy with the upkeep."

"Oh," she whispered after a moment, after realizing she was just standing there.

Just staring at him.

Plastered against his chest, her palm on his cheek.

Ugh.

She yanked out of his hold, pulse thrumming, moisture pooling, and hating herself for turning him down, even though she knew it had been the only thing she could do. "I-I should go."

He nodded, the movement making a flash of tattooed skin appear, just the swirling edge that crept up the left side of his neck. She'd seen that tattoo in the flesh before, when she'd gone into the locker room as he'd been coming out of the shower. Some nudity was a workplace hazard. The guys did their best, but after games they had to shower and change, and if she ventured in, she caught an occasional glimpse of butt or penis, no matter how quick and judicious they were with towels. And, at least when it came to Ethan, those glimpses were usually tucked into her fantasies and paired with her vibrator—because side note: hockey players had the best butts. For the others, they were met with her cheeks growing hot and Dani quickly looking away. Chests and arms, abs and back weren't so bad. She'd almost become desensitized to them, considering the way some of the guys went around without their shirts.

Not *Ethan's* back though. Or his butt. Or his dick. Or his—

Right. She was ridiculously attracted to *all* of his parts, from his mouth down to his strong calves. But back to his . . . well, his *back.* She'd actually felt her heart stop when she'd first seen it— okay, so maybe not *stop,* but it had certainly skipped a beat, hiccupped against her ribs.

Because the tattoos covering his back were beautiful.

Colorful swirls and lines coming together in something that was a cross between flames and floral that combined to form an Irezumi-inspired look. A term she only knew because she'd gone looking after she'd seen them, had researched for hours online until she'd discovered what they looked like.

She wanted to trace them with her tongue, her fingers, her lips.

Had imagined doing that more times than she could count.

"Yeah," he said, and it took her more than a few moments to realize that he'd said it in response to her telling him she should go.

Which meant that instead of continuing to stare at him like a freak, getting lost in those storm-cloud eyes, she *should go.*

Nodding, her embarrassment at a critical level now, she spun away.

And felt him walk beside her, his long stride eating up her much shorter one. She wasn't a small woman by any means, nearly five-ten and a solid size twelve, but he was so big that she felt tiny in comparison.

"What are you doing now?" he asked.

Dani missed a step, nearly faceplanted on the concrete floor.

Ethan, bless him, didn't acknowledge the klutziness, other than to steady her again with one of those big hands—which really just made it even harder to focus on her steps and to not just melt into a puddle on the floor.

"Dani?" he said after a few more moments.

His hand was still wrapped around her bicep, and she found that it was hard to concentrate on anything except the contact.

And that was the only reason she could come up with later for why the conversation went as it did.

"Yeah?" she asked.

"What are you doing now?"

"Um?" She nibbled on her bottom lip. "You mean aside from driving home?"

The ghost of a smile. "*After* you get home," he said. His thumb was on the inside of her arm, tracing lightly up and down, a coil of heat tightening in her abdomen.

Her mouth open and closed. Open and closed.

And then for some really freaking stupid reason, she blurted, "Bath, wine, cold pizza, and bingeing *Bridgerton* for about the fiftieth time on *Netflix.*"

Silence.

His feet slid to a stop, sliding *her* to a stop.

Lightning in those stormy eyes, that thumb pausing, pressing a little tighter. His lips parted and he was close, closer than she'd realized, his hot breath brushing over the skin on her forehead, her cheek . . . her mouth.

Oh God.

Was he going to kiss her?

She wanted that. She *didn't* want that. No, she *needed* his lips on hers.

A door slammed in the distance and she jumped, skittering back, his hand slipping free. Her heart squeezed, and she could feel her pulse thrumming through her veins, thudding against the delicate skin at the base of her throat.

"What's *Bridgerton*?" he asked softly, starting to walk again.

She gaped up at him, frozen in place.

He turned back, lightly snagged her arm again, tugging her forward, and he laughed quietly—a rough chuckle sliding through the air, teasing her skin like velvet and lace running over the surface. That husky laugh joined the imagery of his beard to mentally rub against her thighs.

"What's *Bridgerton?*" he asked again.

"A show," she managed to get out.

"What kind of show?"

The *best* kind of show—strong heroines, gorgeous, tortured heroes, pretty dresses, gossip, and drama . . . and there was that duke. Yum. Because that duke was just . . . her cheeks went hot. "Um . . ."

He bent, nearly running into her for the third time that evening, then his face softened, his eyes danced. "Ah."

She swallowed. "*Ah,* what?"

Ethan straightened, but not before she saw the smile on his lips. "It's a sexy show."

Her lips parted, words stoppered up in the back of her throat.

Yes, it *was* a sexy show, an unapologetic romance that was wonderful to get lost in because was it too much for a woman to want a man to burn for her? No.

But also, *probably,* at least when it came to her.

Sighing, shoving down that sad thought, she knew she'd take her fictional duke any day of the week.

Ethan bent, his mouth very close to her ear. "Want to have a watch party?"

Her throat seized, and she found herself coughing, choking on her own spit. *Ah.* That was another reason she didn't have her fictional duke. Duchesses didn't go around choking on their own saliva.

Ethan's hand slipped from her arm, sliding up her shoulder, drifting to her back, the warm expanse of it running up and down her spine.

"I take it," he said when she'd finally stopped coughing, "that's a no?"

"Uh-huh," she wheezed, turning right at the intersection in the hall and breathing a little easier when she saw the exit to the arena was just ahead. Just a few more steps and she could make her escape from this conversation in which she kept embarrassing herself, get back to her condo, and to her bath, cold pizza, and bottle of wine.

Lucky for her, she didn't have to be on the team's diet plan.

She could self-medicate and ply herself with all the carbs she wanted.

So take that, sexy hockey players with the amazing bodies. She might not have a six-pack—*ha!*—but at least she could eat her delicious crust topped with cheese and sauce and all sorts of other yumminess.

"Dani?"

She jumped, her brain having been locked on the leftovers of her Hawaiian pizza that was currently sitting on the top shelf of her fridge. She could almost taste it—the creamy cheese, the sweet of the pineapple, the saltiness of the ham—and . . . that was not pertinent to this conversation.

"Yeah?" she said.

"Are you scared of me?"

The grizzly bear of a man was touching her, walking close to her, his scent surrounding her, his body towering over hers by a good six inches. He was stronger and outweighed her, and he was certainly way more gorgeous than her—and that wasn't on a hate-herself-vein. That was just pure irrefutable fact. Ethan's cheek-bones were sharp, his eyes unique and intoxicating, his lips kiss-able, and his body . . . well, that was *also* kissable.

Very, *very* kissable.

He made her want to do things that weren't smart.

Very, very *not* smart.

So yeah, he scared her. He fucking terrified her.

A finger brushing along the tip of her nose.

"Yeah," he whispered. "You're scared of me."

"I—"

But what could she do? Argue and deny it? She wasn't a good liar, and she had the feeling that Ethan would see through her anyway.

"Here," he said, in such a gentle way that she immediately felt her spine bristle.

Shy, not fragile.

Quiet, not stupid.

Taciturn, not a bitch.

And what was the point in going down that road again, either in her mind or in this conversation? He wouldn't understand. No one ever did, and it wasn't like she was willing to blab her sad sob story out there.

Or that she had a worse sad sob story than anyone else.

She'd been quiet, not one of the cool, outgoing, beautiful or funny kids. So, she'd gotten her turn as fodder for bullies. It had sucked, but it had sucked for plenty of other kids at her school, and none of them had become this nearly silent, closed down mess of a human that she was.

She was hiding from her life.

Because it was easier and safer and . . . *safer*. That. If she hid, she wasn't vulnerable and could just continue living in her happy little bubble. Could continue to get lost in her numerous video feeds, her computers, her fanciful duke, her cold pizza, and just leave it at that.

"Dani?"

Tone still careful, but marginally so, and the spikes on her spine settled down as she blinked. She realized that Ethan was holding the door for her, and she was just standing there like a freaking traffic pole, staring off into space while he was waiting for her to go out.

Ugh.

Why did he have to be nice?

She wanted to be annoyed but couldn't deny that the chivalrous gesture was a nice one.

Yes, she could open her own doors.

Yes, it was nice when someone—no matter where they fell on the scale of gender—held one open for her.

"Thanks," she whispered.

She walked out. He trailed her, the door clanging closed behind him, and silence fell as they strode across the parking lot. Her car—a small electric sedan that went approximately fifty miles per hour at top speed—was parked on the far end, well away from the players' vehicles, but he still just sauntered along next to her.

"So, what kind of pizza are you eating cold?"

"Why are you here?" she whispered.

Silence.

Tense, painful silence.

It was a sentiment that she'd intended on keeping in her head. It was a sentiment that was probably unforgivably rude, given he'd been nothing but nice and they worked together.

Except for the fact that he asked you out! her inner schoolgirl said. *You don't want to make him mad and then he'll turn on you, he'll turn everyone on you.*

But this wasn't high school.

She didn't have to deal with asshole teenagers.

The team was a family, and even if it was just a family she existed on at the barest fringes—because she wasn't capable of more than that—she was still a part of that family.

They hadn't turned on her.

Yet, her inner cynic said.

He fell quiet at her question. "Do you want me to leave?" he asked, after a moment.

Her car was just a few feet away, and she wouldn't even have to take out her keys. She could just yank at the handle, start her up, and then GTFO.

But the careful way he spoke to her made something inside Dani snap.

People always, *always* treated her like she was weak, like a sharp word might make her cower. So yes, she may be shy and quiet in equal measures, but she *wasn't* fragile. She wasn't breakable.

That had been proven over and over.

So that careful, don't-startle-the-frightened-beast-in-front-of-him tone made her lose her shit.

As in *lose* her shit.

She whirled on him, her backpack jumping off her spine and dropping like a pair of ineffective wings. But she hardly noticed the heavy contents. She was too busy being pissed.

"I am *not* a piece of china to be treated with care," she snapped, poking her finger into his chest. "I am not delicate or fragile or breakable." Each adjective was paired with a poke to his chest—that yummy chest, and the fact that she noticed its yumminess in any form or fashion even while pissed made her even more furious. "I'm quiet." She shook her head. "Yes, sometimes I'm really fucking awkward and shy, but I'm not some crystal vase you have to worry about shattering, and furthermore—"

He captured her finger, held it in that big warm hand. "First," he said, his voice silken. "Yes, you deserve to be treated with care." Thunderclouds in his eyes. "You're a good human being, so you *always* deserve to be treated with care."

Her breath caught.

"Second, I like you shy," he said. "I like you quiet. I like you however the fuck you want to be. So what if you're not crossing verbal swords in the locker room with Max? You're smart as hell, you're funny, even if that sense of humor isn't as loud as other people's."

More breath-catching, more words stuck in the back of her throat. More—

"Third." His voice was velvet again, brushing along her exposed skin and making her shiver. "Third," he said, "is the most important one."

"Why?" she whispered, when he didn't expound on that final reason.

His fingers slipped from hers, shifted up to encircle her wrist, brushing along the sensitive skin on the inside of it and tracing more of those delicate patterns that threatened to melt her into a puddle of goo. Well . . . of that *and* curiosity.

"It's the most important because . . ."

She leaned forward slightly, anxious to hear the answer.

"Another time."

He dropped her hand, and she was despising the loss of that warmth when he stepped around her, opened her car door. Was gaping at his response when he bent—giving her a glorious view of his slacks tightening over that fine ass—to set her backpack in the passenger's seat.

He straightened, brushed the backs of his knuckles over her cheek.

Then he nudged her toward her car. "Goodnight, Dani," he murmured.

She blinked, lips parting, but . . . he was gone.

And she was left wondering—and cursing her curiosity—about reason number three.

FOUR

ETHAN

He'd slept like shit the night before.

Mostly because he'd been dreaming about Dani naked in her bathtub, a glass of wine in one hand, a slice of pizza in the other . . . and also, he'd dreamed about Dani *naked*.

Glorious and naked and *naked*.

Which explained the reason for his cock threatening to crack in half that morning.

He had a great imagination.

Some might even say it was stellar.

Because he could picture every curve, imagine how soft her skin would feel when he kissed his way across it. He'd bet it would be even softer than that on the inside of her wrist, and *that* had felt like silk beneath his rough-ass fingers.

However, none of his imaginings were helping his control.

Or making his morning wood go away.

Groaning as he got out of bed and ignoring the jut of his erection against the fabric of his boxer briefs, he shuffled into the bathroom and turned on the shower, then set about brushing and flossing and getting ready for the day.

It was pretty early by hockey standards—with last night's match start time of seven-thirty, three-plus hours of game play, press, cooldown and stretching routines, and then a shower, it meant that he hadn't left the arena until after midnight. Then he'd come home, reviewed the video, had his beer, and watched the first three episodes of that *Bridgerton* show. He could see why Dani liked it, had felt the urge to keep watching, even after his post-game adrenaline high had begun to fade.

But he had shit to do today, so eventually he'd forced himself to turn off the TV, pried the remote out of his hand, and had gone to bed.

Where he'd slept like shit.

Because he'd been imagining stripping Dani out of one of those prissy dresses from the show and kissing every inch of her glorious body.

After setting his toothbrush on the counter with a sigh, his erection seeming to have no desire to go away, he stripped off his underwear and stepped into the shower. Shampoo, soap, warm water on sore muscles.

A cock that ached for the beautiful, shy woman he'd dreamed about for years now.

It was fucking frustrating.

Not because she'd turned him down when he'd asked her out.

But rather, it was fucking painful that he'd purposely been ignoring his attraction all this time, and then for a few days while he'd worked up the courage to ask her, for a few moments as he'd seen her come out of her office, for *one* conversation when he'd thought that maybe . . . just maybe they might be able to have something that wasn't only work-related.

But that wasn't to be.

"Enough," he muttered. He just needed to ignore his dick, get on with his day, and do his best to forget about one Dani Eastbrooke.

Laughter bubbled in his chest, only it wasn't because the situation was funny. Quite the opposite, actually. His laughter was a product of incredulity because he'd spent two years thinking about her, dreaming of her, and to think that he could just ignore the attraction that had been brewing and growing for all that time, especially now that he'd gotten a glimpse of that fire beneath the cool shield she kept in place between herself and the rest of the world, was ludicrous.

Groaning, he dropped his head to the tiles, felt the cool material against his skin, though it did nothing to tame the need burning within him.

Then he gave in to the inevitable and wrapped his hand around his still-hard cock . . . and stroked, pretending it was *her* hand, that *her* naked body was under the stream, touching him, coming close, her breasts pressing against him, her lips on his—

And he came, her name on his lips.

Fuck, but he was in deep.

Chest heaving, he let the water flow over him, sliding along his back until he started to feel guilty for contributing to the California drought and knew he needed to get on with his day. He cranked the shower off, snagged a towel, and wrapped it around his waist, glad his cock was flaccid but feeling the slightest bit dirty for jerking off to thoughts of a woman who wasn't attracted to him. Then he pushed down the creeper feeling, promised he wouldn't do it again, got dressed, and headed out to get his shit done.

———

The first order of business was the library.

Maybe not the most logical place for a six-foot-five, two-hundred-and-twenty-three-pound professional hockey player, but it was one of *his* places.

Ever since he'd been a little kid, it had been his main happy place.

Tagging along with his parents, disappearing into the children's section while they browsed for research books or just novels to read for fun. He still remembered the feeling of getting his first library card, how excited he'd been to have the power to check his books out, all on his own.

Today, he was filled with marginally less excitement.

He was heading in to pick up some books he had on hold for one of his classes this semester. With hockey as a full-time job and the team's travel schedule intense, he usually only managed two classes a semester. Which meant he was on the four-year plan for his master's, but that wasn't the worst thing in the world. It was the only way he was able to do both of the things he loved—hockey and learning new things.

Plus, he was on his last semester.

If he didn't fuck up, he was going to have his master's in psychology by the end of the year.

What he'd do with it, he didn't know yet.

But he'd have it, and since earning his master's had always been a goal of his—one that had sometimes been at odds with his career, with away games and playoffs and travel—he would be happy just to have the degree to shove in a drawer somewhere.

Then he'd do . . . *something*.

Maybe get a dog, although that would be tough since he was away for half the year. If he wasn't single, if he had a partner like some of the other guys, he could rely on that girlfriend or wife to be on dog duty. Though, he supposed if he really wanted a pup, he could figure it out with a pet sitter or boarding or doggy daycare. But he'd never actually pulled the trigger because it just had never seemed fair to the pooch if he was constantly leaving and coming back. And dogs aside, it was hard to even find someone to date when he was currently hung up on a woman who traveled with the team, a woman he saw nearly every day who made every cell in his body stand up and take notice.

Dani with her beautiful brown skin, those amber and russet eyes, with lips and curves he wanted to kiss—

His cock twitched.

And he forced himself to stop, his hand on the handle of the door leading into the library.

One deep breath, Dani out of his mind.

Another to open the door and go inside.

Immediately, the smell of books wafted forward, drifting toward him, filling his nose and settling that itchy feeling inside him.

The vaulted ceiling overhead was covered in translucent glass, each of the panels surrounded by green metal. The walls were a pale, institutional brown, the carpet industrial and a quite unpleasant combination of tan and forest green, but the book-cases in the distance took the majority of his focus, row after row after row of bottled—or papered, he supposed—knowledge.

He wanted to explore.

But he had more things to do today than just browse through books, as sad as that thought was.

Averting his eyes from the temptation of all those books, Ethan headed to the hold desk and waited in line. A few minutes later, and with a swipe of his library card, he had received his stack of reference materials.

And out he went, thinking about the next item on his list.

Grocery store to pick up Nutritionist Rebecca approved food, the hardware store to pick up some samples of the new floor he was going to have installed. He'd bought it, now that he'd gotten the first long-term contract of his career—six years—and knew he'd be able to settle down in one place.

Plus, the Bay Area wasn't a bad place to live, even once his stint in the league was done.

Whether he'd retire after the next contract (most likely), stay with the Gold, or move onto another team wouldn't be decided anytime soon, but he was just happy to have found a team that he truly gelled with, even if he would never be good enough to be on that top line.

Power plays and penalty kills were his specialty, and between them and with his position as left wing on the third line, he got enough ice time to not hate what he was doing, and to appreciate that offer of six years of stability.

That was a lot more than other players.

Including a lot more than he'd had in the past.

Studying the books in his hands, leafing through the medical journal on the top of the stack, he went to push out the front door of the library when he saw her.

Her.

As always, his heart pattered, squeezing tight, and his fingers went all tingly.

She had a stack of books balanced in one arm, was paging through another . . . as she strode right for him.

He opened his mouth to speak, remembered the tablets, and thought better of it, shifting instead to be in a position to catch, and then snagging her arm. Her head flew up, and he saw that she was wearing turquoise-framed glasses, her hair wrapped up into a loose bun on top of her head, her lips painted a bright pink.

The books tumbled free, but since he was ready, he caught them, pressing the stack between one hand and his side.

"Ethan?" she said.

"In the flesh," he said then winced because *in the flesh?* Who the fuck said *that?* But he was struggling here, he'd never seen Dani in something that wasn't jeans or sweats paired with a Gold pullover or fleece.

This however, was different.

Different as in *incredible.*

Her sundress was giving him all sorts of Bridgerton vibes, even though it wasn't remotely of the era. Rather, he just had all sorts of thoughts about tossing the hem up and losing himself in what was underneath. The fabric was white with large blue and turquoise flowers creeping up from the hem, its hem hitting right at knee level and giving him a view of slender calves, and when his gaze dropped lower, it stuck on pale blue sandals crisscrossing over toes that were painted bright pink.

Fuck, the woman even had beautiful toes.

"Wh-what are you doing here?" she asked.

Since the books were unstable—and not because it would extend this interaction with her—he shifted the stack, tucking them under one arm. "Same as you, I suspect."

Her eyes met his, drifted down in what felt like a physical caress, halting on the stack of research materials he held under his other arm. "You read?"

"I have been known to do so," he said, lips twitching. "Occasionally."

Her teeth found her bottom lip, pressed into that plump, kissable mouth. "I . . . um . . . I didn't mean that like it sounded."

"I know." And he did know that.

Her eyes held his. "I'm sorry."

"Nothing to be sorry for." He started to nudge open the door with his hip, but she slipped past him, held the metal and glass panel wide so he could pass through. "I'm just teasing," he said once they were outside in the courtyard filled with bronze statues of people reading, trees interspaced, their leaves just beginning to change color for the fall, yellows and greens mixing with an occasional orange and red.

They continued walking, this time on the path winding its way to the parking lot. "What did you pick up?"

"Some research material."

She frowned.

"I'm finishing up my degree," he told her, surprised she didn't know, considering the team teased him about it frequently.

"Oh, your bachelor's?" she asked, and he sensed the air around her relax for the first time. His heart thudded. Maybe she was warming up to him. "That's really cool. I know sometimes it's hard for you guys to finish school when you get drafted young."

Ethan spied her car and started walking toward it. "No, actually," he told her. "I was a late bloomer as far as hockey went, so I finished my bachelor's degree before I ended up playing in the league." Which was a good thing. He'd needed those extra years to build his skills, in addition to the additional time to earn his undergraduate studies.

She froze, sandals making a scraping sound on the pavement.

"A master's then?" she asked, brows raised. Her shoulders rose, and though he could only see the side of one cheek, since she was now deliberately looking down at the ground, he knew that she was embarrassed again.

"Yes," he said gently.

Brown eyes sparked when her gaze jerked up to his, and he was reminded again that she didn't like that tone. He couldn't help it, though. There was something about her that made him ache to soothe whatever hurts were inside her, to draw her close and cuddle her tight.

And not in a sexual way.

Though, that was there. That was always there.

He just wanted to keep her safe and then spend the rest of the time making love to her. Also, this just in, he was embracing that feeling from the shower earlier.

He wanted her.

She was here.

He was in deep.

That was just . . . fact.

"I'm a weird one who can't stop going to school." He laughed, mostly so that his cock wouldn't get any harder and he'd embarrass himself.

"No, seriously," she said. "That's awesome. What are you studying?"

"Psychology." A shrug. "Mostly because I want to be able to use my powers to ask all the girls to lie on my couch."

He froze, mortification clawing up his throat, stealing his words. Who in the fuck would say something like that?

Maybe some dumbass frat boy.

But not a grown-ass man, who was trying to somehow win over a woman who wasn't interested.

She reacted exactly as he'd expected, given he'd said something incredibly gross and creepy, and in the simplest of terms, the precise wrong thing to say to anyone, most of all a woman he liked. "Wow, that's really . . . *something*," she said, striding past him, those bare legs gleaming in the sun, the hem swishing back and forth along the backs of her thighs.

"Dani, wait," he said, catching up to her. "I'm sorry, that was . . ." He trailed off, made a face. "I just really fucking like you, and for some reason, I seem determined to put my foot into my mouth every time I open it."

Her eyes studied his.

"I'm sorry," he repeated. "I really didn't mean that thing about the couch. I don't even know what I'm doing." He shoved a hand through his hair. "And the degree is just some piece of paper, some goal I've been working toward. I don't even know what I'm going to do with it, aside from shoving it in some drawer somewhere."

She stilled, those pretty eyes continuing to hold his. Then one corner of her mouth twitched. "It's a good goal, all things considered."

"What's one of yours?"

A flicker of an emotion he couldn't decipher sliding across her face. "I'm boring," she said. "My life consists of testing the latest editing software, pretending to attempt to clear off my TBR, even knowing that'll never actually happen, and eating leftover pizza as much as possible."

God, he wanted to know everything about her. "Is leftover pizza like this Bridgerton thing?"

Her brows drew together. "What do you mean?"

"I watched like three episodes last night." He grinned. "I know what you like."

She spun toward the lot. "No," she said. "You really don't. Not if you haven't seen episodes six, seven, and eight."

Okay, now this was getting interesting.

"What's in six, seven, and eight?"

A flick of her eyes toward his, then back toward the cars.

"Leftover pizza is better than regular pizza because the flavors have a chance to meld, and then when you pull it out from the fridge and chow down on it, those flavors just explode on your tongue." She moaned. "I buy it for the week and have it for dinner cold every night. It's the best."

Cock twitching as he cataloged that moan away for probable shower time later and attempting (and failing) to ignore the whole exploding on the tongue thing, he needed to revisit the ordering pizza for the week, only to store it in the fridge.

"You don't eat it hot?"

She shook her head. "Nope. Put it straight into the fridge and wait until the next day to eat it."

"Wow," he said. "You either have incredible self-control or you're—"

"Incredibly weird?" Her brows flicked, and he got the sense that amusement was tangling with a sliver of old pain. Then she shrugged, and her lips twitched. "Or maybe it's just both, and I should embrace it." With that, she took off across the parking lot, calling over her shoulder. "I'll see you at the rink."

He waited a moment to see if she'd realize she only held the one book she'd been leafing through, that he had her huge pile of —he glanced down, studied the spines—cozy mysteries, thrillers, and romances, but she just kept walking and after a moment, he trailed after her.

She was whispering something under her breath when he caught up, something he couldn't distinguish, but also something he really didn't like the tone of.

"That's why the guys call me Big, Juicy Brain sometimes," he blurted.

Dani nearly jumped out of those sexy, strappy sandals, clasping a hand to her chest and squeezing it tightly. "Will you stop doing *that?*"

"Doing what?"

She plunked her hands on her hips, glared up at him, and Ethan had the distinct thought that when she got mad, she forgot to worry about being shy, forgot about all those things that had her whispering disparagingly to herself. "Sneaking up on me," she snapped.

And yup.

Had definitely forgotten about shy, at least for the moment.

Also, yup, he really, really liked it when she forgot to be shy.

"Just saying"—his lips twitched—"I didn't think nearly barreling you down counted as sneaking up on you."

"Ugh."

Sparks in those brown eyes, and hell if that didn't make joy coil up inside him.

She turned away again.

He followed. Again.

She spun back to face him. "What?" she snapped. "What do you want? Why are you bugging me in my happy place when all I want to do is enjoy my day?" Her eyes narrowed. "With peace and quiet." They narrowed further. "Peace and quiet that doesn't involve certain annoying hockey players."

"How about certain hockey players with your books?"

He tilted his head down, lifted the stack of paperbacks he held under one arm.

"*Ugh.*" She reached for them.

He held onto them, stepping back out of reach. "This is your happy place?"

She froze again. Then shook her head, turned away, and sighed. "You're not going to give those back, are you?"

"Of course, I am."

A glance over her shoulder, and he finally registered something other than sleek bare legs. The turquoise sweater she was wearing was fucking adorable, especially when paired with those glasses and sandals. He was so used to seeing her in casual clothes —sweats, T-shirts, hoodies—that he'd always pictured her in something similar. To see her so girly gave him another intriguing insight. Well, that along with her choice of reading material— which as he glanced over the titles again, he could approve strongly of, even the trio of historical romances that he assumed were inspired by her recent foray into *Bridgerton.*

"What do you mean, of course you are?"

"I mean," he said, "that I'll give them back after I walk you to your car."

Her eyes narrowed.

He nodded over her head. "Let me rephrase," he said. "I've been walking you to your car, and now it's less than ten more feet, sweetheart," he said, "and then you can get rid of me."

More narrowing, more sparks.

And so much less shy.

Months ago, Ethan had already slid down the slippery slope of being infatuated with this woman, but that fire beneath the surface, the sass she was—rightfully—throwing his way . . . well, he was no longer gripping at the hillside, trying to crawl back up. He was plummeting right down into the crevice below and not giving a damn in the least.

He was happy to keep falling.

She twisted to face him again, the fabric of her skirt brushing his bare knees, exposed to the warm fall air by a pair of cargo shorts. But he wasn't thinking of his fashion choices when she stepped close, her chin lifting. "I'm *not* your sweetheart."

"But you *could* be," he murmured.

Her breath escaped on a long, slow exhale. He smelled mint and coffee in the air, was fascinated by the bright pink color of her lips. Had she intended to match her toes? Did she always wear dresses and cute little sandals? Why didn't she ever wear glasses at work? What other lipstick colors did she have? Would she let him kiss all the colors off?

"Ethan," she whispered.

And he would have had to have been inhuman to not love the way his name sounded on her tongue. Maybe that put another tally in the creeper-pervert category, but he was who he was, and the slightly husky tone of her voice as she said his name was the most intense aphrodisiac he'd ever heard.

"Ten feet, love," he said—not gently, not at all, not this time. He didn't want more sparks, more fire—at least not for the next ten feet. Instead, he wanted just a little more time with her. So, his tone was coaxing with a dash of fucking hope.

Because she'd already shot back that fire, forgot to be shy with him, so perhaps getting her to agree to go on a date with him wasn't such a lost cause. But he needed a mix of fire and coax to see if he couldn't weasel his way in with one date. Plus, if he got one—and this wasn't him being an asshole, or not trying to be anyway—he'd bet on being able to convince her to give him more than one.

He could be charming. He was smart, had a decent body, could occasionally be funny.

If she gave him one date, then he had a good chance of securing more than that.

So, fewer flames and more persuading now.

An unpleasant thought welled up within him, because unless, of course, she wasn't attracted to him.

Which would certainly put a damper on his whole plan to win her over.

But he could ponder that later.

In this moment, he needed to take a page out of Billy Madison's book and *get on with the chlorophyll.*

"Ten feet," he cajoled.

She sighed, turned again, and flounced toward her car, that fabric brushing his legs, a silken bite that had him blurting, "Are you not attracted to me?"

Still.

Dani went absolutely still.

And if he were one to congratulate himself on his skills, then he could say that he possessed a unique ability to make this woman freeze in place. As far as life skills went, it wasn't the greatest, but he supposed he needed to take his victories where he could.

She struggled to ignore him.

She shot back fire.

Now, to get that date.

This time when she spun to face him, shock was written into every line of her face—from her jaw to her lips to a little furrow that he wanted to kiss that had appeared between her brows.

"You're asking *me* if I'm attracted to you," she said slowly.

He nodded. "Yup. That's the crux of it."

Laughter filled the air, dancing over his skin, freezing him in place, making him the one playing statue. That clear, hearty sound was fucking glorious, and he wanted to make her laugh again and again.

Of course, he'd prefer if she wasn't laughing at *him*.

But he'd learned over the years to take his victories where he could.

And seeing that amusement in her eyes, hearing her delight, *that* was a fucking victory.

"You . . ." She bent at the waist, the book resting on her hip as she gasped out the laughing words. "Me . . . *Attracted* . . ." More hilarity.

Okay, as time went on, this was less joyful.

"Dani," he warned.

She looked up. "You think *I'm* not attracted to you. To *you*," she repeated. "*To you!*"

Yup, less joyful and more irritating.

"Yes, sweetheart," he muttered. "I think I made myself clear, don't you?"

"No." She tossed up her hands, strode to her car again. "Nothing about this makes sense." Her words came in a flurry. "You at the library. You asking me out. You thinking that you're not the absolute most gorgeous man in all the universe, so freaking beautiful and sexy that I've fucking fantasized about you for *years*. I mean, your tattoos, your butt, your *abs—*"

She clamped a hand over her mouth.

Meanwhile, he was processing.

Processing.

Beautiful and sexy and gorgeous and . . . *fantasized?*

About him?

"Oh, my God," she moaned, the words muffled through her hand. She dropped it. "Please, tell me I'm in a horrible dream, that I didn't actually just say that out loud."

He couldn't bite back the smile. "Fortunately, for me, no, we're not in a dream."

She pinched herself on the arm. "*Ouch!*"

Ethan took a step toward her, wanting to grab her hand, to stop her from hurting herself again, but his arms were full of books. "What'd you do that for?" he muttered.

She moaned again, one hand coming to her forehead, the other still clenching the novel at her hip. "Not a dream. Not a dream. Oh *God*, not a dream."

"Dani?"

Shaking her head, she whirled around and went directly to her car, yanked at the handle and started to climb inside.

He hotfooted it over to her, managing to slip into the opening before she could slam the door shut. The metal panel collided with his hip. "Didn't you want your books?" he asked when she didn't look at him, just slammed the door against his hip once more.

A sigh, her body going still.

Then she released the door.

He crouched. "I like your dress."

"Books, please," she said, twisting to hold out her arms, though her eyes were deliberately away from his.

Ethan separated his from the stack then handed hers over.

"Dani?" he asked again.

She spent an inordinate amount of time stacking them on her passenger's seat.

He waited, had the feeling that he would wait for however long this woman needed. Of course, the alternative was that she run him over or barrel through the parking lot with her driver's door open.

Though, he supposed, given the weight of the glare she tossed his way, neither of those options was out of the realm of possibility.

"You're attracted to me?" He set his books on the roof of the car.

She groaned, plunked her head against the steering wheel. "Why?" she moaned, banging it enough times that he finally reached out and captured her shoulders. "Why, God," she moaned, her eyes sliding closed, "are we still having this conversation?"

He held on to her. Waited.

She peeled back her eyelids, glared at him again. "Did the whole drooling over your abs and tattoo thing not clue you in?"

A smile tugged at his lips.

Another groan.

"What?" he asked, brows drawn together.

"That." She waved a hand at his face.

"*What?*" he asked again.

"*That,*" she muttered. "That smile peeking out at me like it's the best freaking gift I've received all day. It's just a smile. I shouldn't like a freaking *smile* so much."

"But you do?"

Her eyes sparked, and she sighed heavily. "Do you have an ego problem or something? You need someone to constantly be building it up?"

A shrug. "Better than it being constantly pricked."

She sighed again, then said, "Why are you tormenting me?"

"Because I have questions."

Another glare. "Well, *I* have errands."

His lips twitched. "Me, too."

She waited.

"What errands do you have?" he asked.

A muscle pulsed in her jaw, just beneath the edge of the bone, at the top of that kissable expanse of neck. He could almost feel the tremble against his mouth, wanted to dart his tongue out to taste the flicker.

"Dani?" he prompted.

Her fingers clenched on the steering wheel. "Grocery shopping."

"What else?"

Her shoulders crept up. "Nothing."

"Sweetheart?"

"Not your—"

"Sweetheart," he interrupted. "Right. Sorry."

Her lips pressed flat.

"So, what else?"

There was that pink again.

"What?" he pressed.

"I should go."

Okay, now his curiosity was seriously peaked. But he was seeing that this woman was stubborn, that she wouldn't give in easy. Which, of course, made her all the more interesting, especially considering this was the longest conversation they'd ever had. "What are you buying?"

Her brows drew down, another V forming.

"At the grocery store," he said, anticipating her query. "What are you picking up? More cold pizza?"

He watched her throat work as she swallowed. But then her chin lifted, her tone growing clipped. "Food, Ethan," she muttered. "I'm buying food that isn't pizza."

"Me, too," he said. "I'm going to the store to buy food, too."

This was definitely not a charming exchange, this definitely bordered on inane and nonsensical, and yet . . . he was having a fucking ball.

"And then what?" he asked. "After the food, you're going . . ."

Silence. Long and drawn out and . . .

That chin lifted again, the amber in her eyes flared with fire. "And," she snapped, "now we're circling back to why are we even having this conversation?" Her eyes were on his, not disappearing over his shoulder or sliding down to her hands. Just fierce brown eyes holding his . . . and he fucking *wanted* her.

Bad.

"I don't know," he admitted.

Other than the fact he was in deep . . . and loving every minute of it.

"So, you'll be going?" she asked, the question so expectant that a curl of wickedness coiled through his abdomen, slipping in alongside the need and affection. She might as well have asked, *"So you'll be coming inside me?"* for how his body reacted.

He liked her like this—her expression arched, her eyes on his, that shyness slipping away so he could see the fierce woman inside.

He rose to his feet. "You're right."

That froze her again, the plump, kissable pillow of her bottom lip separating from the top, a flash of bright white teeth as she scrambled to comprehend his sudden agreement.

As tempting as it was to lean in, to taste that mouth, he gave into wicked.

Well, wicked that wasn't having him take liberties in the parking lot of a public library.

Smiling, he stepped out of the opening between the door and car, snagged his books, crossed around the front, picked up *her* books, and crammed himself into the passenger's seat of the tiny sedan.

FIVE

The *click* his seat belt startled her out of her shock.

"What—"

Ethan spun toward her, and for a moment, she thought he might tug her into his arms, yank her across the console, and kiss the shit out of her.

She would have liked that, too.

Not that she would have admitted it.

Because even though this man was beyond gorgeous, even though she burned for him, she dreamed and fantasized and touched herself pretending he was hers, that wouldn't ever be.

He would destroy her.

It was as simple as that.

Despite that, she still wanted him to kiss her, still wanted to feel his body against hers, his hands on her skin, his cock thrusting deep. Throat going dry, her fingers actually cramping with the urge to touch because the thought of him inside her was intoxicating and dangerous when this man was so close—close enough that her pussy throbbed, that her nerves were on fire, that—

He didn't kiss her.

He just set the stack of books on the back seat and faced forward again. Then calmly asked, "Would you like me to drive instead?"

"Wh-what?"

His hand came down on top of hers, squeezing lightly where it rested on the steering wheel. "Are you okay?"

Such an absurd question, she thought.

Of course, she wasn't okay.

She was nowhere even near it, and how *could* she be when this man was so close, the spicy scent of him filling her car. She could smell the mint of his toothpaste on his breath, and it mixed with the tang of pine, the faintly biting, briny notes of the ocean. His smell made her want to move closer, to forget about *him* tugging her over the console and instead, to climb over it herself, to straddle his hips and—

"Whatcha thinking?" he asked, his fingers squeezing hers lightly.

And that little convulsion, the warm, rough hand engulfing hers . . . well, it had the last of her filter dissipating like so much smoke.

Which was the only reason she could account for later for why she just straight up blurted, "How much I want to fuck you."

The air in the car went taut.

"*What* did you say?"

She was horrified, slowly dying inside, that death agonizing, a painful millimeter-by-millimeter creep until she had to physically stop herself from yanking open the door and running screaming through the parking lot.

It was *her* car, for God's sake!

"You should go," she whispered.

He didn't move, except to squeeze her hand again, to unwind it from the steering wheel and bring it across the console.

"Eth—"

Her palm suddenly made contact with a hard cock . . . with *his* cock. Her fingers involuntary clenched, and he groaned.

"Dani?" he gritted.

"Yeah?" she breathed, her hand starting to move.

"I want to fuck you, too."

Her throat seized. "I'm seeing that," she forced out.

"But," he said, gently peeling her hand away and lifting it to his mouth. The bristles of his beard tickled her palm, his tongue a hot brand. "I'd like to get to know you a little better first, okay?"

She was feeling a little dazed, and her words were equally as stupefied. "By grocery shopping?"

"Yup." He smiled.

Her brain short-circuited. The sun was shining through the window, gilding his skin, bringing out a lighter blond, almost red undertone in his hair. His teeth were bright white, though she knew that the one, two right of center, was fake. He'd been hit in the mouth with a stick during the playoffs last season, and even through the mouth guard he wore, his tooth had been knocked out. Instead of doing what any sane person who'd just lost a tooth would have done, he'd played the remainder of the game *and* the double-overtime periods (during which he'd also scored the game-winning goal, NBD). But anyway, by the time a dentist had been able to get a look at him, it had been too late to save the tooth.

So, a fake one.

Which was a mental tangent she shouldn't be going down right at this moment, with Ethan in her car, smiling at her, saying that he wanted to go grocery shopping with her of all things.

But the things she *should* be doing didn't always factor in with what her mouth did.

Case in point, that instant.

"Did it hurt?" she asked.

His smile drifted away slowly, like a cloud floating across the sky, the wind morphing its shape, flattening it on one corner, dragging it up on the other . . . and then she blinked. Or maybe like when she'd been a kid staring up at the clouds, finding crea-tures and telling stories in the white wisps trailing over the cerulean blue, the sun got into her eyes, making her squint, and all of a sudden, the story was gone, the smile flattened.

But the potential of a new saga could be found in its place.

Fingers on her cheek. The lightest brush of his thumb across her cheek.

"Grocery shopping?" he murmured.

Her lips curved. "Your tooth."

That pulled his hand from her skin, his pointer finger tapping the fake tooth. "Yeah," he said. "It really fucking hurt."

Dani raised her brows, surprise a tiny bolt of lightning zigzagging across her spine. "It did?"

His smile returned, and she found herself searching the lines, the bristles of hair surrounding it, the pink lips, the flash of white teeth for a different story . . . and found it, she supposed. She'd expected a macho reply, something about it not hurting because he was a big, tough hockey player who could take pucks to the body, sticks to the face, checks into the boards, and regardless of blood or bruises or teeth falling out, he got right back up, hopped straight onto the ice for his next shift.

"Yeah, it did," he said, his gray eyes flickering with amusement.

"Oh."

Silence. Then a light tap to her temple. "It looks like you have more questions in that big, juicy brain of yours."

Nope.

The questions had all flitted away to subspace, twinkling along with the stars, pretty, but impossible to grab on to.

"That's your nickname."

His smile was a physical gut punch. "You pay attention."

Mutely, she shook her head.

"No?"

"You just talk a lot."

He froze, and then his laughter filled the car, filled her, made her unstick or perhaps become somehow even more entranced, because she was absolutely rapt by everything this man did—the way his throat worked as he chuckled, his big, scarred hands clenching on his thighs, that mouth tempting as it curved.

More silence. Another brush of his thumb on her cheek. "Should we get on with the painful adventure known as grocery shopping?"

"You don't have bags," she said.

To his credit, he didn't misunderstand about the local law that charged for using anything that wasn't a reusable bag in stores, instead he just shrugged. "I'll buy some."

Her lips parted as she mentally searched for a way to get him out of her car. Mostly because she wanted him so much, and that made him dangerous for her sanity and the well-being of her very jaded heart. "That seems very wasteful."

"Unless you have some I can borrow?"

She didn't. She'd brought the precise number of bags she would need for her weekly trip for junk food with the odd vegetable thrown in. Probably, she could lose a few pounds if she ate more of the latter and less of the former, but she didn't care.

Once upon a time she *had* cared, and that had been disastrous for her mental health.

Now, she ate her fucking Oreos and didn't give a damn if her jeans weren't a size zero.

Instead of getting into her whole woman-hear-her-roar situation, Dani just simply said, "No."

For some reason, that made his lips twitch.

"Why don't you have any?" she felt obliged to ask.

A shrug. "I was going to walk home for them."

Her mouth formed the word *walk*, but even though the sound didn't cross her lips, he still saw or heard it or maybe the man who made her nipples tingle, her thighs quiver, maybe he just had fucking superpowers.

That seemed the more likely scenario when he said, "I live around the corner."

"Oh," she whispered.

"Want to come home with me, so I can grab some and not be *wasteful?*"

She swallowed. Hard. Hated that she felt like she was trapped inside a washing machine, being jerked this way and that during the conversation, not able to feel like she was in the least bit of control, not even for a moment.

She knew she could kick him out, could continue to feel stuck and whirling every time she had a conversation with him. Or—

Or she could just embrace this conversation, the time with a man who was funny and a little pushy and who'd also saved her books from hitting the ground. She could accept that out-of-control feeling and just live for *one* fucking moment.

By grocery shopping.

Yup.

Even when she was pushing her boundaries, she was living a huge, exciting life.

Paper or plastic.

The proverbial question.

Six

Ethan

He could freely admit that he was shocked she'd said yes.

Completely and utterly shocked.

But instead of wasting his opportunity, he used his hockey player skills to think quick on his feet and give her directions to his place.

It was a little over a mile, tucked on the edge of town, up against a creek. With neighbors on just one side, it afforded him the quiet and privacy he craved, but it wasn't so far from the small downtown area that he couldn't walk to the restaurants and shops a few streets over.

For him, it was the perfect fit.

Also, because he was south of the city, real estate prices weren't so bad, and for a player who'd been shuffled around quite a few teams before he'd found his fit (thus contract offerings hadn't been filled with outrageous professional athlete money), less expensive housing prices were right in his wheelhouse.

She pulled into the driveway, completing the short trip in a way that was much what he would have expected—competent, careful, with no extraneous movements.

He waited until she put the car in park, until she'd gotten out, before he grabbed his books, popped the door, and led the way up to his front porch, watching her as she took in his little house. It was a neat Craftsman two-story home, sitting on a decent-sized lot. The front yard was small with a tiny patch of grass and some planters on one side of the driveway, a curved path leading up to the door. The back yard was nice, though. Good sized and shaded, plus as a bonus, the previous owners had left behind their hot tub.

Immediately, thoughts of coaxing her into that steaming water, her curvy body clad in a skimpy swimsuit, had him distracted and way too ahead of himself.

But that was him with Dani, wasn't it?

She paused on the porch, and he waited for a moment for her to go inside before he remembered she *couldn't* go inside.

Because he had the only key.

Dumbass.

Stifling a sigh, he unlocked the door and held it for her to walk through.

Her quiet studying continued as she stepped into the hall-way, as she glanced at the pictures he had lining the wall on either side. He saw her lips curve, her hand lift to point at one of his mom's favorite photos—him amongst a giant stack of books.

"It's come to you naturally then," she said softly.

He chuckled. "That it does. Both of my parents are giant nerds."

"You saw my stack of books. What does that make me?"

"A nerd." He tugged a lock of her hair. "But an adorable one with obscenely sexy toes."

She froze. "What do you mean?"

"I *mean*," he said, "that your toes are sexy."

Dani spun for the door.

"What are you doing?" He placed his hand on the panel before she could open it.

"You've apparently got a foot fetish," she said, "and sorry, but that's a step too far for me."

"I don't have a foot fetish," he said, stepping close. "What I do have is a *Dani* fetish, and that includes sexy dresses and toes and turquoise glasses."

Her brows dragged together. "You like my glasses?"

"And your feet." He leaned against the door, his shoulder against the wood, his chest facing her side. It was convenient because he was able to study her *and* prevent her escape. Muhahaha. "Though, not in a creepy way. Now, going back to the glasses. I haven't seen you wear them before."

A blip of something—no, of *pain*—in her eyes. "No, I . . . um . . . wear contacts at work." A shrug. "After the game last night—" She shook her head, stopped talking, and he waited a few moments for her to finish the thought. When she didn't, he pushed away from the door, took her hand.

"What happened after the game last night?" he asked, drawing her down the hall.

"Nothing," she said, dropping her chin to her chest and studying the woodgrain of the floor. "I fell asleep with my contacts in. That's bad, and my eyes hurt this morning, so I wore my glasses today."

He studied her face, the tendrils of pain clinging to the edges of her expression. "No," he said. "No, that's not it."

Her brows raised. Her hand slipped from his.

He amended. "Or, at least, that's not *only* it."

"I thought we were getting to know each other over food shopping," she said, turning back, her eyes drifting over the pictures again before she reached the opening to his kitchen. "This isn't the grocery store. Your bags in here?"

"No."

She spun to face him, lifted a brow.

"Want to elaborate?" he asked. "A pregame to the getting-to-know-you grocery talk?"

Her throat worked, panic in the depths of her amber and russet eyes.

"Or how about I just grab the bags?"

There.

He saw the exact moment she relaxed, her shoulders settling, her lips curving just the slightest bit. "You snoop," he told her, "I'll go out back and grab the bags."

"Out back . . ." he heard her say, but the words disappeared off into space when he slipped through the back door. His garage was detached and abutted the yard. Having been built later than the original house, it was plunked into the back corner of the lot. He didn't mind the short walk most days, though it sucked hauling shit into the house in the rain.

Luckily, this was California, and rain wasn't a common problem.

Still, at that moment, he quickly strolled across the yard, certain that she wouldn't just abandon him and his apparent foot fetish.

Why, one might ask?

He grinned.

Because he held her purse in his hand. Which conveniently held her car keys.

Another muahaha.

He strode to his car, grabbed the reusable bags from the trunk, and strolled back in time to peek through the back windows and witness Dani snooping, or maybe not something quite so obvious. Rather, she seemed to be slowly studying each corner of the space, as though it were an art exhibit and she needed to take in every inch.

He waited for her to make a circle, to return to facing the back door, and her reaction when she completed that turn, when she was staring at him through the glass, did *not* disappoint. Her lips parted, and he'd bet this cute little house that her cheeks would be hot. Behind those turquoise frames, her eyes widened, and she clamped a hand over her chest.

Ethan tugged open the door. "Whatcha doing?"

To her credit, she got over her surprise in a flash. Shrugging, her tone completely even and without a hint of embarrassment, she said, "Snooping."

"That usually involves opening and closing things," he said, moving to a bank of drawers and tugging out the top one. "Like that." He nodded at it. "This exhibit is my junk drawer, and there are many interesting things in here that tell you about the various parts of my psyche."

Her lips twitched, probably because he sounded like a dumbass.

But whatever, she wasn't running from the house, so that was a win in his book.

"Like what?" she asked, peering down into the drawer.

Okay, that he wasn't really sure of. It *was* his junk drawer, a place to dump his receipts, old keys, etc. His gaze drifted down, and also apparently a place to dump several candy bars and a manual for his car. He reached in, picked up one of the bars. "I like Snickers?" he asked.

More twitching of those lips. "That is not on Rebecca's meal plan."

Probably why they were shoved in the drawer in the first place. "How about receipts?" He snagged one at random. "Look, this says I spent twenty-two dollars and ninety-six cents on gas."

She giggled. "That is actually more telling than you probably suspect."

"Why's that?"

She snagged it, pointed at the total. "It means you're one of *them.*"

"What do you mean by *them?*"

"Them being," she said, lips twitching, "one of those weirdos who fills up their car when it's only halfway empty."

He tilted his head to the side, and he studied her closely. "As opposed to what?"

She set the receipt down, closed the drawer. "As opposed to us normal folks who drive until we're on fumes and then begrudgingly hit up the gas station."

"That sounds stressful."

Amusement in those amber eyes. "I like to live dangerously." She laughed. "Okay, not so much. The truth is that I hate going to gas stations."

"Why?"

A shrug. "It just always seems like such a waste of time. The cheap places always have long lines, and then it takes forever to fill up your tank, but not long enough to be able to do anything productive like reading."

"Bookworm," he teased.

"Takes one to know one."

He laughed. "Also, not sure if you're aware, but you're obsessed with this concept of wasting."

She smiled up at him. "I like to be as frugal with my time as possible, is all."

Curiosity threaded through him like fibers weaving into a basket, coiling, wrapping around each, pulling taut. "And what does being frugal with your time consist of?"

Her gaze drifted to the ceiling as she considered the question. Then she glanced back down, her eyes meeting his, and it was as though he'd been struck by a cattle prod. Electricity flowed through his nerves, his muscles tightening, his body going stiff— okay, maybe that was just his cock.

"Keystrokes are the most important frugal use of my time," she said, "followed by doing my best to never drive during peak hours, thus wasting my free moments in traffic." She ticked off the items on her fingers. "Also, I never spend more than eight hours in bed, even if I can't sleep."

He'd circle back to that later—because there were many reasons to spend more than eight hours in bed, especially with a woman like Dani. Right now, he had to bite on something else she said. Lifting a brow, he asked, "Key . . . *strokes?*"

A chuckle bubbled up in her throat, and she sighed. "Seriously?"

He took her hand in his again, lacing their fingers together, tracing light patterns on the inside of her wrist. She shivered as he touched that sensitive skin, but she didn't pull away. In fact, she shifted a little closer. He sidled closer himself, until his body was a hairsbreadth from hers. Her skin smelled like strawberries, and he found himself drifting closer, wanting to taste it on his tongue.

Patience.

"So, you never laze in bed?"

She swallowed, and he traced the lines of her throat with his gaze. "No," she said. "I don't have any patience for it. Too much to do. Too many things in my brain that . . ." She trailed off.

"That what?"

"Too many things that only seem to come to the forefront of my mind when it's too quiet, when dark has taken over the world." She shook her head. "That sounds ridiculous, I know." A smile that didn't look right in the least. "Come on," she said, turning for the front door, "let's go get food."

"Sure," he said, keeping his tone deliberately light, wanting to tug her out of whatever had made her sad. He could tell she didn't trust him enough yet to share what had wounded her so deeply. Instead, he teased, "I'd be happy to go on a date with you."

She sputtered, spun back. "I—uh—"

"What's the matter? I'll be a cheap date when you're paying, I promise." His lips curved. "Most of the time, I'm only allowed to eat vegetables."

Dani shook her head, eyes wide, and arms stuck straight out at her sides.

He walked to her, not stopping until his toes were millimeters from hers. "Dani?"

There was a bead of perspiration on her throat, sliding down beneath the neckline of her dress, down between a pair of some of the most gorgeous breasts he'd ever laid eyes on. He could see her pulse thrumming, just above her collarbone, a tiny fluttering of butterfly wings.

"I wasn't asking you out," she whispered.

"I know." He took a chance, bypassing the miniscule touches, the barely there brushes, and cupped her cheek. "I am," he said. "Asking you out. At some point in the future, when you're guaranteed to say, yes," he added when he saw the protest begin to gather on her face.

Her sigh coated his skin, and for a moment, she leaned into his hand, her body drifting close enough that the tips of her breasts whispered across his chest. "I don't know that I will," she breathed.

His hand flexed on her cheek. "I do," he said.

There was something between them. He felt it. *She* felt it.

The same *thing* that had prompted him to invade her car and go grocery shopping together. The same that had her lingering near him, her body leaning toward his. It was an invisible thread, slender and reedy, but it was the promise of something different than he'd ever experienced.

Something that had him pushing forward when he would have normally backed off.

Because Dani was different.

She drifted a little closer, her chest brushing his, those glorious breasts barely making contact. It was a fucking tease, that light contact, and the urge to yank her close was intense.

But instead of giving in to her, he shoved that down, stepped back, and asked, "Groceries?"

Her chest rose and fell, her cheek slipped from his hand, and . . . a trickle of ice slid down his spine.

Because eclipsing that thread was the refusal he saw in her eyes.

Fuck.

"Or if not groceries," he said quickly. "Then maybe—"

He froze when she touched him, her fingers combing lightly through his beard, sending prickles of sensation down his throat, his torso, unseen fingers wrapping around his cock and squeezing tight.

"It's soft," she whispered. "I expected it to be rough."

Ethan didn't dare move, not when she was touching him with such feather-like strokes, not when it felt so fucking good. Not when—

She stepped back.

"Groceries," she murmured.

He wanted to wind his fingers into those sleek brown curls, to haul her flush against him, and to kiss her until they were both reduced to ashes. To forget all about the need for oxygen and food and . . . whatever other things humans needed to survive.

But . . . groceries.

So, he stuck the bags under his arms and let Dani lead the way out the front door.

Seven

Dani

She stared at the bags of groceries on Ethan's arms, one after another hooked on his big arms like giant bracelets hanging from wrist to elbow.

"Mandy"—one of the Gold's trainers—"is going to kill me if you get hurt because you were carrying my groceries," she murmured.

"Mandy," he said, smiling up at her with that fucking gorgeous grin that never failed to turn her insides to jelly, "will understand that sometimes a man needs to take care of a woman—"

"How incredibly sexist of you," she said dryly.

And who knew that *she* could be dry? Well, not in the non-wet sense, because she spent the majority of her time in that non-wet manner (aside from Ethan's effects on her pussy . . . *ha*), but rather in a witty, sarcastic way. She was usually so worried about all the jumbled thoughts in her head getting mixed up and tangled, those lame, mismatched bits trying to escape and rendering her unable to form a sentence, let alone any banter or a droll comeback.

But with Ethan, it was different.

Somehow, all the voices in her head expounding on everything wrong with her, all the mistakes she'd made, the stupid things she'd said, the embarrassing stuff she'd done . . . quieted when she was with Ethan.

"—*he* cares about," he said, continuing his silliness about a man needing to take care of a woman he apparently cared about, "no matter if she's strong and capable enough to carry in her own groceries."

She crossed her arms. "And *your* groceries? Should I carry those in turn?"

"My groceries will survive my walk back to my place."

"You're going to *what?*"

"Walk," he said, pausing by the door to her condo and waiting while she unlocked the door and held it for him, after shifting the single paltry bag he'd "allowed" her to carry after she'd pitched a fit, in order to stick the key in the lock and open it.

Also, that was new.

The fit part.

That she somehow felt comfortable enough with Ethan that she could argue with him. Aside from her mom and dad and two sisters, she didn't argue with anyone. She kept her head down, tried not to draw attention to herself, and lived her life to the best of her ability.

No.

The last part was a lie.

She lived her life to the best of her ability to keep herself safe.

That was to say, she hid.

From nearly everyone and everything.

Long-term relationships? Hell, no.

Friendships? Few and far between. She considered herself closest to Stephanie, or Fanny as she preferred to be called, who was the Gold's skating coach, but that was a new friendship, still fragile and building, and she wasn't sure she'd ever be able to open up enough to find the closeness a piece of her deep inside craved.

Aside from Fanny, she'd even resisted being folded into the friend group of the Gold woman, until Mandy had physically dragged her to one of their girls' nights out.

She'd had a nice time, and the women were all awesome.

But it was already hard for her to get a word in edgewise in a normal conversation, let alone with a group of beautiful, successful, smart, and funny women who *weren't* shy.

Dani did better one-on-one, and she did even better when that one-on-one was with a person or people she knew—like her parents or her sisters.

It was easier to get a word in when she remembered that Toni had once puked all over the carpet because she'd eaten too many bowls of Cocoa Krispies, or that Loni (yes, her parents had a thing with names ending in I) had once nearly burned down the house because she wanted to teach her hamster to jump through a tiny flaming ring.

Also, let it be noted that no hamsters were harmed in the training of said trick.

The curtains in their living room, on the other hand, had been permanently scorched, and the paint—freshly done by their mom—hadn't fared much better.

She could easily talk when she remembered that her mom had once broken her big toe because she'd gotten so mad at the washing machine that she'd kicked the clear plastic circle on the front—not once, but three times. And she could tease her dad about his inability to start campfires, even when provided with accelerant, a lighter, and dry wood.

Because she had years of memories, the comfort of all that time, and the fact that they'd stuck by her when things went to absolute shit.

It was just the rest of the world she couldn't trust.

Maybe that made her pathetic, but she'd been burned deeply enough to not be willing to put her happiness and mental well-being on the line.

Better to live in the small, happy world she'd created.

But with Ethan—who had walked past her and into her tiny kitchen and was currently stacking the bags on the counter—she was tempted to make that world a little bigger. She wasn't . . . well, she wasn't exactly comfortable with him. *Definitely* not comfortable. Instead, she was—

What?

Uncomfortable? Yeah, sure.

But also intrigued by the gentle, quiet, tamed grizzly bear way he'd managed to draw her into conversation, entranced by his smile, the kindness in his eyes, utterly, hopelessly captivated by the pushy—and yet somehow still charming—way he'd hijacked her afternoon, coaxed her into shopping with him.

She couldn't remember the last time she'd relaxed enough with a person she hardly knew, let alone a *man* she didn't know well, to actually laugh with him.

But she'd laughed with him.

A lot.

While walking up and down the aisles of a grocery store.

And . . . she had liked it, liked laughing with Ethan, liked spending time with him, liked *him*, plain and simple.

Did she like him enough to want to expand her little bubble of safety?

Maybe . . .

Her heart twisted, convulsing rapidly, sweat sheening the back of her neck as she considered, as she wondered, as she *wanted*. But ultimately, her old habits were too ingrained.

No. She couldn't risk it.

Even if he was handsome and charming, pushy and as cuddly as a teddy bear, she couldn't just put everything she'd worked for on the line for one man, and most especially for a man she worked with.

That was . . . stupid.

And no, that wasn't disappointment coiling through her at her decision, sinking into her bones, making her hate that safety net she'd erected. It was sensible relief that she'd chosen to keep that barrier in place. It was. *Really*, it was. Sighing, she finally unstuck enough to move forward through the wide entrance to enter the kitchen, opening her mouth to tell Ethan that she'd drive him and his copious amounts of vegetables and plant-based proteins back to his house when she got out of her head enough to process what he was doing.

What. He. Was. *Doing.*

Her fridge was open, and he was stashing the groceries neatly inside. The junk food—more than normal, since she'd both panic-bought during the first half of their shopping extravaganza and then had thrown way more than she'd needed into her cart when he'd begun teasing her about killing herself with all that refined sugar.

Spite carbs, that was what she'd blown her grocery budget on.

But, she thought, eyeing the stash of cupcakes and chips and pretzels and cookies, the spite carbs were totally going to be worth it.

He had put away all those carbs—okay, well, he'd efficiently lined up all the boxes, bags, and trays of junk food—on her kitchen island, a veritable smorgasbord of delicious sugar and artificial flavorings.

"Dani?" he asked, turning from the fridge, a bag of apples (See? She didn't buy *only* spite carbs). "You okay?"

Her throat seized, a haze settling over her—a mix of terror, hope, being touched by the simple act, and then more fear, knowing this would only end one way, and desire. And still, all she wanted in that moment was to not care that she already knew how it would end.

She wanted to find the courage to see it out anyway.

All because a man put her groceries away.

She was fucked. Completely and utterly fucked. Because that bubble had expanded without her permission, had shot forward to encompass this man and . . . now circling back to the fact that. She. Was. *Fucked.*

So, no, she wasn't okay.

How could she possibly be okay?

She spun, hustled from the kitchen, moving—okay, *running* straight down the hall and out onto the tiny little patio that was beyond the back door. Her chest heaving, she leaned back against the cool wall and sank down into a crouch, gripping her hair.

She couldn't do this.

It was fucking reckless.

Playing Russian roulette with her heart, just offering it up for him to pull the trigger over and over again until the bullet would inevitably fly through the air and tear through the organ.

Like it had before.

Fingers on her wrists, gently but inexorably tugging them away from where they held her hair.

Ethan didn't say anything, but Dani's eyes were open, staring first at the ground, then at the toes of his boots peeking into her periphery. He didn't say anything, just waited. Probably for her to give him some explanation for why the sight of him putting away groceries had caused her to turn and run.

Disgust slid through her.

Hating that she was like this.

So freaking bad at life, at people, at . . . normal fucking human reactions.

"I'm not good at people."

The fingers on her wrists began moving, tracing slow, light circles on her skin. It shouldn't be a sensitive spot, not when that area spent the majority of its time resting against a keyboard, but the gentle touches set her nerves firing, made goose bumps prickle and rise, the hairs on her nape lift.

"What do you mean, sweetheart?" It was a low, husky question, one said so carefully that it slid under her defenses, threaded its way right through the gaps in the mesh of her safety net.

She shook her head, tugged her wrists free of his hold.

Her skin tingled, even after his fingers slid off, a phantom imprint of his touch lingering long after he'd sat back onto his haunches and waited.

The silence stretched—a taut, uncomfortable thing—reminding her of trying to wrestle herself into a too-tight swimsuit in a dressing room, squirming and jumping, tugging and wiggling it up, until it finally engulfed her from shoulders to hips, squeezing tight on her lungs, her stomach. Nausea coursed through her, burned the back of her throat.

"For the record, I think you're doing just fine with people," he said.

Dani froze, then her gaze flew up to his. Laughter bubbled up inside her, escaping out through her nose in a semi-painful snort. She sank down further, her butt hitting the concrete of the patio, her head resting back against the house. "You're delusional if you could possibly think that I'm good with people."

"Just because you don't interact in the same way as others doesn't mean you're not good."

It took her a minute to puzzle that out.

Then her brows drew together, her head shook. "You really are delusional."

One half of his mouth quirked up, but his tone was easygoing as he sank down opposite her, matching her position on the concrete. Its coolness was seeping through the fabric of her dress, making her shiver, or maybe that was just because he rested his hand on her ankle.

"Okay?" he whispered.

Throat going dry, she thought about the contact, knew that she should say she wasn't okay with it, just out of principle. But . . . the truth was that his large, warm hand resting on the bare skin of her ankle felt nice.

More tendrils slipping in through the gaps in her net, winding their way around her insides, filling her with warm, fluffy cotton candy straight out of the machine. Sticky fingers, the puffed sugar melting rapidly on her tongue, its sweetness bleeding over her taste buds, sinking down into her stomach, and all of those dopamine receptors in her brain blazing happily to life.

"Dani?"

Still wrapped in that warm, fluffy dopamine feeling, she found herself nodding.

The other half of his mouth curved, joining the first. Then he stretched out, leaving his hand where it was, even as his legs bracketed hers.

Bare skin brushing hers, the rough velvet of hair-covered male legs making her shiver in the absolute best way.

"Cold?" he asked, eyes soft and curious.

Since she wasn't about to admit that she was ridiculously attracted to those legs, to the dark hair covering skin that was tanner than she'd expect for a man who spent the vast majority of his time indoors, she just simply said, "No." Then hurried to ask, "Do you spend a lot of time outdoors?"

His brows lifted, perfectly framing gray eyes that were such an interesting mix of the shade—steel-colored with faint streaks of blue, a charcoal outline around his pupil. He didn't comment on her staring, on her random question, just nodded and smiled again. "Yes, after freezing my ass off in an ice rink for most of the year, I really like soaking up the California sunshine." A beat. "Do you?"

Her teeth found her bottom lip, nibbling, a stupid fucking nervous habit that she hated, one she immediately pulled back on, releasing it as she shook her head. "You saw the pile of books I picked up from the library, what do you think?"

"I think," he said, his fingers flexing slightly on her ankle, sending heat curling through her, though he didn't move any closer, "that you are the type of woman who can do whatever you want, whether that's kicking ass behind the computer, hiking to the top of Mt. Shasta, sailing around the Bay, or just spending the night in the bath with a book and bottle of wine." He smiled. "And that slice of cold pizza."

She laughed, but it sounded off because shock had sliced its way through her at the words, at what this man thought she could do, what she might *like* to do. Was there ever a person, even her awesome family, who'd told her she could do everything? *No.* She was used to people putting her in a box, to hearing, "you're a nerd because you like to build computers and game the night away, so there's no way you'd want to scale a mountain or sail around a body of water." Maybe the bath, wine, and reading would fit into their preconceived notions, but the rest of it?

No.

Not so much.

And that wasn't even touching on the numerous microaggressions—and oftentimes the aggressions that *weren't* micro-sized—the real-life discrimination and hate that came from being a woman of color in this world.

Even if she put that aside and focused on her nerdy qualities, on the things she'd been bullied for, Dani had always figured the rest of the world saw her as a woman they expected to have a trio of cats named Austen, Brontë, and Dickenson, and to have her *Harry Potter* house tattooed somewhere on her body. (Also, yes, she was a Hufflepuff and had a tiny badger inked on the arch of her foot, but her cat in high school had been named Nora, after the queen of romance, not the others. Neither of which were important to the topic at hand, except to say that she'd lived so long considering what the world thought of her, what box they tucked her neatly into, that it was both odd and refreshing to have a man seemingly allowing her the space to define herself).

It won't last.

Her inner voice was a major fucking buzz kill, even as she acknowledged that it was probably right.

There was a reason for her safety net.

A reason she'd decided to get really good at keeping her safety net intact.

Even aside from the bullying that came from being a girl interested in tech, and a Black girl at that, she'd been burned enough times by friends and love interests after high school to know that her inner buzz kill spoke the truth.

His interest wouldn't last. He would put expectations on her.

He would try to make her fit into those, to act a certain way, would twist and change and . . . *hurt* her.

That was why this was so dangerous.

Why her longing, that bubble expanding, that safety net wanting to unravel . . . why all of them were so terrifying. Because she wanted to undo everything for Ethan. But what did he want in return?

The man hadn't paid her any notice for two years, and now, after a handful of conversations, a couple of touches, and a few hours together, she was ready to melt for him, to let him in.

If he really wanted her, why had it taken him so long to take notice of her?

Except . . . she wasn't exactly an open book, was she?

Keeping people well enough away from her was kind of Dani's superpower. Right up there with making things really freaking awkward.

Case in point? Now.

"I have a badger tattooed on my foot," she blurted.

His gaze dropped down, fingers sliding along her ankle. "Where—*ah*"—his finger swiped along the arch of her left foot—"I see it," he murmured. "He's cute." His hand stayed on her foot, brushing lightly over the inked animal. "So, you're a Hufflepuff?"

Swoon.

Fuck, this man was treacherous for her heart.

"What are you?" she asked.

His smile twined around her insides, squeezed tight. "You don't want to guess?"

She rolled her eyes. "I don't have to guess," she said. "Without a doubt, you're a Gryffindor."

That grin widened. "Nope."

Her brows rose, shock weaving through her for a second time. "You're not a Gryffindor."

A solemn shake of his head. "Nope."

Except . . . there was something on his face that prickled her instincts. "Oh my God," she said, sitting up. "You're messing with me." She tucked her knees under her, cupping his cheeks in her palms. "You're totally a Gryffindor."

His hands covered hers. "Yeah. I'm a regular lion."

"A grizzly bear," she murmured.

"What?"

"You're like a giant, cuddly bear, who—" His thumb traced lightly over her bottom lip when she stopped, breath sliding out.

"You're so beautiful," he whispered, his mouth coming close.

God, he was going to kiss her, and she wanted it so badly, and—

What if he's different?

He's not, she countered. *He can't be.*

She sat back and stood, his hands slipping from her face. "I should drive you home."

She wasn't going to look at him. She *couldn't*. Because she couldn't allow more seepage into her net, couldn't allow any additional melting or bubble-expanding. But for all her best intentions, her eyes were drawn back to his.

Protest in the gray depths had her steeling her spine.

He stood, took a step toward her. "I figured I'd call a Lyft," he said, near enough that she could feel the heat of his body. But he didn't touch her again, and she spent a moment processing the disappointment swelling in her like a balloon attached to a helium tank that wasn't shutting off.

Growing larger and larger.

At *her* for not being brave and opening herself up to new experiences. At him for making her want those new, dangerous life events.

Swelling, the latex growing dangerously thin.

He brushed a finger across her bottom lip, gray eyes searching hers. "Yeah, I'll call a Lyft."

Then he was gone.

And she found herself sinking back down onto the patio, listening for the front door to close behind him.

When it did, she tried to convince herself that the balloon inside her didn't *pop* in time to that soft *click*.

But all that convincing didn't make one bit of difference; regret flooded through her, sinking heavy through her limbs as the sun descended and she finally managed to push herself up from the patio, heading into the house and seeing . . . the pile of her books stacked neatly on her counter.

Junk food.

Books.

And . . . a bottle sitting on top of a note.

Thought of you when I saw this.
Hope you get to enjoy a bath tonight.
-E

Bubble bath.

She popped the top, inhaled.

Strawberries.

The same scent as the lotion she slathered on every morning because she absolutely loved the way it smelled.

And the same scent Ethan had noticed enough to buy the corresponding bubble bath.

Dani's eyes slid closed.

She wasn't disappointed. She wasn't. She *wasn't*.

Anyway, even if she was, she understood herself well enough to know she'd get over it.

EIGHT

ETHAN

The hit came out of nowhere, smashing him into the boards hard enough that all of the air squeezed out of his lungs, his shoulder colliding hard with the glass.

Everything went out of focus for a heartbeat, but then he was shoving the opposing player back, kicking the puck forward and out of his feet, getting it back on the blade of his stick and forcefully carrying it out of the zone.

They were on the penalty kill, down a goal late in the third, and their players were tired.

He needed to get the puck over that blue line, get it deep enough into the other zone that they could change for the second penalty kill unit—the next group of his teammates, who would try to kill off the other team's one-player advantage.

But they weren't going to make it easy on him as he bodily shoved himself forward.

A hard swipe of the fucker's—aka a player from the other team's—stick against his hands, sent a stinging pain crawling up his arms. He'd had much worse, though, so he didn't falter, successfully creeping up the final six inches and getting the puck out of the zone. Now, the other team had to all clear out, and they had a little breathing room. Enough at least for him to be able to glance up, to see Max streaking forward, looking not the least bit tired, even though he'd just worked his ass off in front of Brit's net.

Ethan banked the puck off the boards, tapping it around the player trying to intercept, unconsciously holding his breath until it was on Max's stick and his teammate was skating down the ice.

Then, even though his lungs were burning, he sprinted to the bench, allowing Coop to jump over the boards and join the rush. It was two-on-two, but then Blue joined in, exiting the box as the penalty ran out, and the Ducks made a bad change, and in a second, the Gold had numbers with their opponents scrambling to get back into their end of the ice.

A pass skipped over Blue's stick was scooped up by Coop, who made a move that was all kinds of illegal (in a strictly that-was-fucking-amazing and not that it-was-against-the-rules-of-the-game way). He crashed the net, faked a shot, and passed it back door to Blue, who didn't miss a beat as he slammed it home.

The crowd erupted, the walls of the Gold Mine seeming to vibrate with the roars of pride and happiness (and occasional boos from the few Ducks fans in the stands), and for a moment, Ethan wasn't present in the game.

He was wondering if Dani was able to hear the cheering deep in the bowels of the arena, where her office was located, if she'd seen the play, seen him working hard.

Pathetic.

Certainly.

But maybe if he couldn't win her over by hijacking her afternoon of reading and librarying, then maybe he could impress her with hockey skills.

She liked the sport.

Right?

He supposed she had to, given how much of it she watched.

Which brought him back to hoping she'd seen it, even though

he knew that she was probably busily reviewing angles in case the goal was challenged, labeling different portions of the video feed for review later. He also knew that sometimes she ran behind the actual game play, using the commercial breaks to tag all the various things the coaches wanted earmarked so they could be pulled and stitched together after the game or in between periods.

Still, his ego wanting to be boosted aside, Ethan knew Dani was working her ass off right at the moment, so he pushed all thoughts of stroking (sweet Christ, why was he always thinking about stroking with that woman?) aside and glanced down at the screen placed beneath plexiglass below the bench, the goal replaying over and over again from various angles.

He watched Coop's move again—fuck that was sick—and then was surprised, his eyes drawn from the screen when Bernard, their head coach, tapped him on the shoulder with the rolled-up sheaf of papers he always carried when coaching. Considering he'd never seen Bernard look at them, Ethan thought it was the older man's version of a fidget spinner. Not that he'd ever voice that thought aloud. Players didn't rock the boat with their head coaches.

Or at least not players who wanted to actually get a decent amount of ice time.

He met his coach's gaze, forced away thoughts of fidget spinners.

Bernard nodded approvingly. "That was you." Another tap, and then he was back focusing on the rest of the team, talking with the ref, saying something into Calle's—their assistant coach, who had a killer mind for offense (and also Coop's wife)—ear before focusing back on the ice.

Which was what Ethan should be doing.

Except, now he wasn't just wondering if Dani had noticed his role in the play, but whether she'd caught Bernard giving him props—something that was rare with their typically quiet coach and something that had his post-goal grin widening.

Probably not.

She had a million things going on at once.

But when he happened to notice the camera on him, spotting part of his face on the monitors beneath his feet, he lifted his head, stared directly into that lens and winked.

Hopefully, it was so fast that no one but Dani would have seen—he doubted this but was prepared to take any teasing tossed his way, regardless—

The ref blew his whistle.

Ethan focused on the ice.

The puck dropped.

The game went on.

And all thoughts of winks disappeared, but the notion that Dani might be watching stayed in the back of his mind, had him skating harder for those final few minutes, had him working his ass off as they wound down and the play moved into overtime. It had him positioning himself in the right place at the right time when he took his turn, accepting a pass . . . and stuffing it past the goalie.

Then as the horn blared and the crowd cheered, as his team-mates surrounded him for the requisite hug, her presence stayed there.

Maybe she hadn't seen the wink.

But hopefully, she had seen the goal.

NINE

A wink.

God, it should have been dorky as all hell.

But instead, she'd nearly swallowed her tongue, had almost gasped out loud, both somehow at the same time, which would have been critically embarrassing considering Jess was in the room with her.

She could hear how the conversation would go in her head.

Why are you choking on your gasps, oh boss of mine?

Because I'm a dumbass, who nearly swooned over a wink.

Of course, Jess would never call her *oh boss of mine*, but that was far from the point.

The point being, of course, that Ethan had winked.

At her.

And she'd gotten all fluttery inside.

"Fucking hell," she whispered.

Sliding, sliding down that slope, the rope of her safety net fraying more by the second.

"I know," Jess said, her eyes on the screen. "That move was incredible."

"Yes." She focused back on her job, filing the wink to deal with later, and then added, "Coop has great hands."

Jess grinned over her shoulder. "Too bad he's madly in love with Calle, because those hands"—she clasped her fingers together, air-kissed them, a la chef style—"though Ethan isn't too bad. I wouldn't mind feeling that beard between my thighs."

This time, Dani did choke on her gasp, coughing as she attempted to capture the continuing play. "That's"—*cough*—"not"—*cough*—"very"—*cough*—"professional."

Jess grinned. "I forgot we did that here."

Dani snorted. "You know I'm not mad, it's just . . ."

"Shitty and reductive?"

A shrug. "Maybe."

"Probably." She tossed another smile over her shoulder. "I'll be on my best behavior from here on out."

Another snort, mostly because Jess was never on her best behavior, and that was part of the reason it was so fun to spend hours in the booth with her. "You forget I know you."

"You forget . . ." She scowled. "You're right."

Dani laughed.

Then they both got back to work, playing catch up at times as they broke each play down into tiny bite-sized pieces to be consumed later. But by the end of the game—and after a really nice goal from Ethan—the Gold had won, and they were packing up.

"Nice work," she told Jess, as her assistant shrugged into her coat.

Jess nodded. "It'll still be nice to get an actual intern to help us with the busy work, but we've got a good system down."

"Agree completely," she said, running the clips through a backup program. "But I'm back to the drawing board on that after our last debacle."

"We'll be good until it's sorted."

And with that, they hashed out a few details for the next game —an away one—before Jess slipped out into the hall.

Dani, meanwhile, waited for the backup program to run, even though she didn't strictly need to, since it was all automated. But she wasn't quite ready to head out into the hall, on potential collision courses with men who winked at her.

At *her*.

Because it *had* been for her, right?

"I mean," she whispered, swiveling in her chair, running her fingers over the keyboard, and really wishing she hadn't already eaten her one box per day limit of Hot Tamales during the game. "We spent all day together yesterday. He said he wanted to date me. Who else could it have been for, if not me?"

"It was for you."

Her breath caught, and she swiveled in her chair. Ethan stood in the open doorway, freshly showered and looking all too tempting.

"What are you doing?" she asked, when he stepped inside and closed the wooden panel behind him.

"If it's my dorky ass wink that you're referring to, that is." He smiled, and her brain melted. Just like that.

"Ethan," she murmured.

He sat in Jess's chair, wheeled it close. "Do you have any video for me?"

"I—um—" She sucked in a breath, released it slowly. "I don't have any video for you. Jess took care of that tonight."

"Good." He rolled closer until his knees were on either side of hers. "You okay?"

She swallowed. "Why wouldn't I be?"

"You were upset yesterday," he murmured.

No, she had been overwhelmed yesterday, frustrated at herself, scared that she liked this man so much.

That was the painful and unhappy truth.

She was the problem, not him.

"I wasn't upset at you."

He slid a little closer. "I know."

And . . . silence.

Good times. Happy times. Fucking awkward times.

"I'm not going to ask you out again," he began, causing her eyes to fly up from the pale pink she'd painted on her fingernails, matching the color he'd mentioned liking on her so-called cute toes. He wasn't going to ask her out? But what if she wanted him to?

Wanted him to?

Fucking hell.

She needed to get her head in shape before she even began considering whether or not she wanted the man to ask her, and how she might answer him, how fucking awkward she would be on a date if she *did* happen to agree to go with him.

God, because if she agreed to go out with him, then she would have to consider what she wore, what she said, what she—

"Would you kiss me?"

His gray eyes widened, the pink tip of his tongue darted out and tasted his bottom lip. "Dani?"

She shoved her chair back, stood, and moved to the door, intending to yank it open, to create an escape route—although her fuzzy brain wasn't telling her if it was an escape route for him or for herself—but then Ethan was there. Right there, pressing her front into the wood, his chest and torso hot and hard where it brushed her spine.

"Do you want me to kiss you, sweetheart?" he breathed into her ear, the bristles of his beard running over her jaw, making her shiver.

"I—I didn't mean now."

"No?" He rested his hand near her head, his hips resting heavier against hers.

"N-no," she murmured. "I meant on a date."

He inhaled sharply, body going still. "Yes, baby, I'd most definitely try to get a kiss, if you agreed to go out with me." The words were hot and damp, reminding her of other parts of her body that were hot and damp, reminding her of parts of *his* body that could play nice with those hot and damp parts of hers.

His lips brushed lightly over her skin, and then she didn't have to imagine what the prickles of his beard would feel like.

Glorious, was the answer.

The stubble had gooseflesh rising on her nape, had her hips arching back and pressing against the hard jut of his erection.

"Fuck, Dani," he murmured, that beard sliding lower, his lips trailing along her throat. "You are so fucking sexy."

"I—" She didn't know what she was planning on saying, probably something mood-killing about how she wasn't sexy, how she was too fat and frumpy and too fucking shy to be sexy.

But then he . . . sucked.

His lips pursed on her skin, sucked lightly, and Dani could have sworn that she melted—just turned right into an ice cream encountering the mid-summer sun, turning into a puddle as it dripped down its cone.

"Will you go out with me now?" he murmured.

Her hands clenched, and for a moment she didn't process that she'd reached behind her, was grasping onto his neck and shoulder, her breasts lifted, pleading for his attention, her fingers of one hand plunging into his hair, those on the other digging into the hard muscle of his deltoid.

"I—"

His hips were flush to her ass, his cock hard, and she grew even wetter as his hand trailed up her side, stopped just beneath where she wanted it, fingers running lightly over the bottom edge of her bra.

He nipped at the spot where her shoulder met her throat, and she jumped, spinning in his hold, wanting to see his face, needing to deduce what was in his expression. In the blink of an eye, the move had her against him, had her front pressed to his front, and fuck having an up close and personal view (and touch) of Ethan Korhonen was a damned good thing.

"Is that a yes—"

A knock interrupted his question.

"Ignore it," he whispered, his fingers tugging the collar of her shirt to the side, his lips and tongue and beard driving her slowly insane.

"Dani?" A voice called.

Except, it wasn't just *a* voice. It was Fanny.

Nosy, pushy Fanny.

Ethan cursed, pushed off her, plunking into a chair and somehow able to look cool, calm, and collected, even though she was still that cone full of melted ice cream, liquid leaking out of her and turning into a puddle.

Another knock.

Ethan pushed out of the chair, took Dani's hand and led her to her seat, pressing her down into it. "It's unlocked," he called, picking up a tablet and appearing in an instant as though he hadn't just been practicing giving her hickeys on her neck.

The handle turned, and Fanny came in, her gaze alighting on Ethan and then Dani, brows raising into sharp little rainbows on her forehead. "Am I interrupting?"

Ethan stood. "Nope," he said, voice calm and friendly. "I'm just returning this." He held the tablet out to her, his expression relaxed, though when his gaze met Dani's, his eyes held a heat.

One that she knew was mirrored in her own.

Then he was gone, and she was trying to convince herself that she wasn't disappointed she hadn't gotten to answer him, hadn't felt that stubble on her lips.

Nope.

Not disappointed.

Relieved.

That was what the sharp, jabbing pain in her heart felt like.

Relief.

Yup.

Yup.

Fanny sat in the chair Ethan had just vacated, and Dani felt a bolt of annoyance that her friend was there instead of the man she was lusting after. But then Fanny began expounding on her latest exploits as a thirty-something woman trying to find a man who wasn't a total freaking loser and . . . seriously, she could relate.

Except . . . Ethan wasn't a loser.

So, yeah, she was disappointed and annoyed—at herself.

Stifling a sigh, she tuned into Fanny's words, knew that she owed it to her one friend to pay attention.

But it was a struggle.

Because she couldn't help but feel that she was utterly, royally fucked to the moon and back.

But it'll be a fun, fun ride, her inner daredevil—the one that was usually stifled by her anxiety, her fear—said.

Until it's not, the sane part of her countered. *Until it's not.*

TEN

I t was almost time to get on the ice.

It was their last match at the Gold Mine before a six-game road stretch. Not that Ethan minded the trip. He wasn't leaving his family behind or a significant other. Actually, the whole trip was a net positive for him because his parents were coming to the game in Baltimore, and he was excited that he'd be able to hang with them for a day. Usually, the team only played their Eastern Conference opponents twice during a season, so he was glad his parents could make it out for one of the match-ups.

Not that he was like a little kid desperate for them to come and watch.

Rather . . . he was like a little kid excited to show off his new toy—and that toy was *not* Dani (she'd be fucking terrified if it was, though he couldn't deny he hoped to at some point get her comfortable enough to be folded into the Korhonen crew). Instead, his excitement was because he was with a team who valued him, who gave him ice time and the opportunity to play, and his parents would see that. It didn't matter how many games they'd already come to over the course of his career (and they made it to a half-dozen a year), Ethan still got a thrill from them watching him play in a *Gold* game.

They weren't coming to watch him sit on the bench like teams past.

They'd see him living his dream, on the ice, hopefully making a positive difference for the team.

They'd see him doing something productive, something *important*. Though not as important as their jobs, their teaching and research, at least when he was on the ice and not warming the bench, he was actually doing something that came close to the value they brought.

Which was why as much as he wanted to get his degree, as much as he knew that he was smart and capable of getting *that* degree, he'd always had a hard time reconciling what he did with what his parents did. They loved him, he'd never doubted that. It was just . . . sometimes being the jock son of two renowned professors made him feel like he was a pair of sneakers amongst a whole row of expensive high heels.

Couldn't measure up.

Didn't measure up.

Wouldn't *ever* measure up.

Smothering that feeling, shoving it deep down where it managed to live most of the time, he slammed his car door shut and started for the arena, but then his nape prickled, and he slowed, turning back toward a row of cars on the far end of the lot.

Because his inner Dani detector was ringing.

He walked over to her, watching for a moment as she wrestled with a series of bags in her trunk. Then he moved closer, some part of him pleased when she froze and rotated to face him. No surprise on her face, just expectation. "Ethan," she murmured, her eyes meeting his and flitting away.

He'd had his mouth and hands on her, knew how silken her skin was, knew that she tasted of strawberries and cream. "Let me get those for you."

"Oh, no—"

Ignoring her, he hefted the totes, surprised to find they were so heavy. "What's in these?" he joked lamely. "Bricks?"

"Actually," she said, trailing off, her lips quirking up.

"Wh—" He peeked inside one of the bags, knowing it was rude but doing it anyway, and saw that while there weren't bricks within the sturdy canvas, there *were* rocks. Lots and lots of rocks.

She opened the one light bag he hadn't managed to wrestle away from her, showing him that inside were a few bottles of paint, along with some brushes. "PR-Rebecca had a doctor's appointment, so I offered to pick up the supplies for the newest Miner's Club activity.

Miner's Club was a group for any kid thirteen and under who was a Gold fan, and the PR and Community Outreach teams worked together to have fun crafts and activities in the concourse before puck drop for every home game. The kids loved it, and they especially loved that a lot of the projects they worked on ended up in the community.

Case in point, Dani saying, "They're painting rocks that will line the walkway of the new senior center."

"Make sure to slip in a few Gold logo rocks," he said lightly.

"You have any doubt that PR-Rebecca doesn't already have that planned out?"

He laughed, waited while she closed the trunk and locked her car. "Do I look like an idiot?" A grin. "I'd never doubt PR-Rebecca."

Dani stopped, eyes locking onto his. "No," she said. "You don't look like an idiot, you look like—"

She pressed her lips together.

He was dying for her to finish that statement, but a muscle in her jaw was clenching, her gaze deliberately turned away.

"What are you going to paint on your rock?"

Her fingers played with the strap on the bag and as they approached the door to the arena, he thought she wouldn't answer. But then she did, her voice quiet but steady. "What makes you think I haven't already painted some?" She reached into one of the bags, pulled out a rock about the size of her palm. "Here," she said, holding it up. "This one is my favorite."

The pale gray stone had been painted a bright white, several turquoise and blue flowers covering its front and back.

It reminded him of her dress from the library, the gleaming umber skin, the bright pink of her toes, the way it had felt to touch her, even if it had just been on her ankle.

He wanted it.

Wanted to take it from her hand and shove it in his pocket and to never, ever give it back.

But . . . he wasn't about to steal from senior citizens.

"There. You see?" she asked, her hand closing around the rock and tugging the door open. "I did a mediocre job throwing a few examples together so that Rebecca wouldn't have to." A smile as she waited for him to pass her. "I get my gold—no pun intended —star for the day."

"I didn't think techies liked arts and crafts time."

"Are you kidding?" she exclaimed. "We love arts and crafts time, or at least this techie does." A shrug. "Anyway, it was nice to do something that wasn't screen-related, at least for a little bit."

"It's beautiful," he told her truthfully.

Her stare came to his, held. "I don't know about beautiful," she said. "But I like drawing anyway."

"*You're* beautiful." Despite the bags, he managed to brush her fingers with his.

"Eth—"

He stepped closer, ignoring the fact they were standing in the doorway, blocking the entrance that any number of people needed to use, a doorway in which any number of those people could stumble upon them, all of whom would certainly spread the news about how they'd seen him mooning over Dani right where anyone could see.

But he found he didn't care.

Not with the scent of strawberries on her skin wafting up to tease his nose. Not with her eyes on his. Not with her adorable nose and kissable lips and the heat of her body very close to his.

The only thing he *didn't* care for was that his hands were full.

He couldn't touch her properly, couldn't tug her close, couldn't stroke them over her body, couldn't—

"What are we talking about?" Max.

Ethan held back a groan, shifting forward so he was out of the doorway, even as Dani all but jumped out of her skin in order to dart out of Max's path. "We're just delivering supplies for PR-Rebecca's Miner's Club project," he said calmly before she could sprint down the hall. "She's the brain. I'm the brawn."

Max chuckled, patted him on the arm. "Every once in a while, you can be amusing."

"And you try so hard but never actually succeed at it."

Dani chuckled.

Max clamped his hand over his chest. "I'm wounded."

"You'd have to have a heart for that," Ethan grumbled.

"Oof," Max said. "I'm doubly wounded."

"Liar."

"True." A beat. "Except about the heart stuff. Mine is huge, some might even say big and juicy, like *someone's*"—he took advantage of Ethan's full hands to scrub one of his over the top of Ethan's head and mess up his hair—"big, ole juicy brain."

Ethan managed to whack him in the kidney with one of the bags, which he considered a successful response to all the big and juicy stuff.

"Oof," Max groaned, hand pressing against his back. "You wound me."

"I *can* wound you," Ethan muttered.

"Children," Mandy warned. "What are you arguing about?"

"Ethan's trying to hurt himself," Max whined, "by carrying heavy stuff before game time."

Mandy glanced at the bags then at Dani, who at that moment stopped trying to melt into the wall and instead jumped into action by trying to snag the load from him. He held onto the bags, ignoring her efforts even as Mandy snorted. "Seriously?" the trainer asked. "*That's* what you're coming at me with?" She tapped her finger to her chin. "I think it's a thigh massage for you."

Max paled, and Ethan didn't blame the man. For one, Mandy's thigh massages were strictly for medical purposes and weren't what most of the populace would consider relaxing. Rather, they were beyond firm, beyond deep tissue, and more than a little painful—she called them physical therapy with a purpose, and that purpose seemed to be torturing. For another, the person who actually gave them—the team's masseuse, Darby —was tiny but with freakishly strong hands.

Hence the talk of torturing.

At that moment, however, Mandy was doing less torturing and more snooping. She moved toward him, peeked into the bags. "Oh, is this for the rock activity?" She released them, walking next to him as they continued down the hall. "Madeline"—her daughter—"is all about the need to get paint *everywhere*."

Dani's throat worked, but Ethan didn't rush her—and to their credit, neither did Mandy or Max—each just waited as they strode through the hallways winding through the underbelly of the arena. "I put together a bag for the team kids to be taken up to the Family Suite," Dani eventually said, gaze flicking to his, then to Mandy's. "It's the one with the otter on the front."

Ethan's heart squeezed.

Lovely woman.

"Aw," Mandy said. "You're amazing. They're going to love that."

A shrug. "I know it's a little hard for the team kids to get upstairs sometimes, especially when they don't want to take away from anyone else's experience."

That was true.

It sometimes put the players' kids in an awkward situation, wanting to participate in the fun but not wanting to be seen as taking something away from the other kids.

"Anyway, I thought they'd enjoy it, so I figured I'd make it easy for them to participate," she finished.

"You're sweet," Mandy said, reaching across Ethan and squeezing her hand. "Do you want to take the bag up yourself?" Dani's feet faltered, and with Mandy's arm still extended in front of him, he was nearly clotheslined. Luckily, he stopped just in time, bags swinging forward and back.

"No," she whispered. "I—I—" A breath as she fumbled. "No, I've got stuff . . ."

"I can bring it up and give it to the babysitter who's in charge tonight?" Mandy asked when Dani trailed off. "Would that be easier?"

Gentle had crept into Mandy's tone, and he watched as it flowed through the air, as Dani processed it, her shoulders going stiff, her chin lifting. "No," she said, "I can take it."

"Are you sure?"

That chin rose further, and Ethan could have sworn that he heard her teeth clack together. "I'm sure."

Mandy nodded, pulled her hand back, and they began peeling off—Max into the gym for a pregame workout, Mandy into the training suite.

"Where do we need to take this?" he asked once they were alone.

"PR-Rebecca's office." A clipped statement. "Then the otter bag upstairs."

"Do you want me—"

"I *said*, I was going to take it up."

He stepped in front of her, forcing her to stop. "I was going to ask if you wanted to take the otter bag up while I dropped the other stuff off to Rebecca."

She skittered to a stop right in front of him, and he jerked to a halt, the bags colliding first against his body then against hers. "Oof," he muttered as rocks jabbed into his hip.

Dani winced. "Sorry," she whispered.

"No, I'm sorry. You okay?"

She shook her head. "I'm a mess."

"Because of me or the rocks?"

More halting, more shaking off her head. "Because . . ." A sigh. "Of me."

He studied her face, not liking the tinge of misery creeping into the edges of her eyes, clouding the amber and russet with cool steel, pulling those plush lips flat. "Well, if it counts for anything, I think you're a gorgeous mess."

She glanced down at herself, made a face. "I'm in jeans, a baggy fleece, and no makeup."

He set the bags down, tapped her temple. "I meant in here."

Laughter bubbled up in her throat, burst out from those kissable lips. "How in God's name could you possibly think that I'm beautiful in my head?" She threw up her free hand, the bag on her wrist keeping her other at her side. "That mess I'm talking about is *in* my head. I'm so screwed up from stuff I should be over that it's not even funny."

ELEVEN

One second, she was standing in the hall, readying to spill her guts to Ethan, and the next, the bags were on the floor, including the one hanging on her wrist. Before she could even suck in another breath, she found herself with her spine pressed to the cool wall, Ethan to her front.

And it was glorious.

It reminded her of the almost-kiss.

Reminded her of his mouth on her throat, his hands on her body.

"You don't have to justify the way you feel to anyone. Your past, painful or not, is what makes you Dani." His head dropped. "And from what I know of Dani, you're pretty fucking special."

Was it possible for her heart to beat its way out of her chest? Because with his silken voice in her ear, with the gruff *pretty fucking special* reverberating through her body like a ping pong ball zipping from rib to rib, it felt on the verge of doing so. Three words and she was ready to spill her guts—

No.

She'd been ready to spill her guts before.

Now, she was ready to let him in, to allow that safety net to peel back and take up trapeze as a hobby.

And *that* had her heart pounding for a whole other reason.

"I'm just Dani," she whispered.

"I know," he murmured, cupping her cheek, brushing his thumb over her bottom lip. *"Just Dani*, I really want to kiss you right now."

Her inhale was a sharp stake driving into the ground, or maybe the gasp one takes right before letting go of the trapeze bar and leaping to the next. "I'm—"

Voices trailed down the hall, echoing through the mostly concrete space, snapping her out of her Ethan haze—and seriously, the man was fucking dangerous to her mental aptitude.

He didn't move, just leaned his hips a little heavier against her, and she felt his erection, hard and unyielding and so fucking tempting, pressing into her stomach, before his mouth dipped down and and he whispered roughly in her ear, "Tell me you're dying to have my mouth on yours, sweetheart. Tell me that you're wet, that you're aching for me as much as I'm aching for you."

Her eyes flew up, caught the storm in his, his desire lightning strikes through the deep gray. "Ethan," she breathed.

Because . . .

Yes, to *all* that.

The need, the aching . . . the wet.

She wanted him more than she'd ever wanted anyone, and that was less about her and more about the invisible, persistent thread that connected them, a spool that wound tighter and tighter until—

His hand clenched on her hip.

His mouth came closer. "Do you want me?"

"Yes," she murmured and watched his features tighten, his eyes spark, his lips move—

The voices drew nearer.

"Fuck," he cursed and shoved back, bending to snatch the bags up just as Blue and Coop came around the corner. Brows lifted, probably because she was still against the wall, her chest heaving, hand pressed over her heart. "Here." He shoved two bags at Coop, another two at Blue. "Bring these to PR-Rebecca's office."

Blue opened his mouth.

Ethan pointed at him. "Not today, kid."

"You realize that we're the same age, right?"

"I'm older," Ethan grunted.

"Barely," Blue countered, but then he shut up, hefted the bags, and turned around, heading back where he'd come from.

Coop hesitated, a bag in each hand, eyes on Dani's.

She nodded.

One half of his mouth turned up.

And then he, too, headed for Rebecca's office, the bags clutched in huge, capable hands. Ethan slipped the otter one around her wrist, patted her hip, gaze still scorching, still making her ache to have his lips on hers. "Take these upstairs before we get caught making out in the hall like teenagers."

She wrapped her fingers around the strap and nodded, unabashedly watching him grab the final two bags, his strong, powerful thighs stretching the fabric of his slacks, his ass perfectly accented against the thin gray fabric.

She'd said it before, and she'd say it a hundred times more.

Hockey players had the best asses.

He turned, suddenly very close again, his voice the best kind of husky, his beard brushing her jaw, teasing her skin, need coiling inside her like a taut hose refusing to stay in place. Instead, it kept bursting forward, causing her fingers to tingle, her breath to catch, her thighs to clench.

His lips pressed . . . to her forehead. "I'll see you after the game?"

A shuddering breath, her bones threatening to melt.

"Dani?" he asked when she just stared.

She managed a nod.

That got her a sexy smile before he turned and headed down the hall, giving her another glimpse of his gorgeous ass as he went.

She was seeing him after the game.

Squee!

Shit.

But . . . *squee!*

Also, best. Asses. Ever.

Also, she bit the inside of her lip, watched as he turned the corner, hoping he liked what she'd put in his pocket.

———

She was riding high from the near kiss in the hall, the memories that normally made her cling tight to her safety net easing, fading into the background where they belonged. So much so that the anxiety that usually gripped her when dealing with people hadn't swarmed up and overwhelmed her as she'd walked into the Family Suite.

Kids and wives, fiancés and girlfriends filled the room with a kind of happy cacophony.

"Dani!" Sara called as the door closed behind her. "It's so good to see you!"

Sara was married to Mike Stewart and was close to Brit and PR-Rebecca. Dani had met her on more than one occasion, and the former figure skater was a genuinely nice person.

Today, Sara set down her pencil and sketchpad (she was also a talented artist) and crossed over to Dani, taking her hands. "How are you?"

Warm.

Sara was just really nice and warm.

"I'm good," she said. "I just brought some craft supplies from the Miner's Club for the kiddos."

A squeeze of her hands. "You're so sweet." Sara's smile had garnered many a sponsorship. "Do you want me to get it set up so you can go get ready for the game? I'm sure you have better things to do than wrangling team kiddos."

"Oh, um, sure," Dani said, relinquishing the bag, a sliver of disappointment sliding through her. She'd thought to hang out a little bit. She wasn't needed downstairs quite yet, and kids were always easy. Honest to a fault, but mostly a judgment-free zone.

Mostly judgment free because the last time she'd been up here, Aiden—Blue and Anna's son—had told Dani that she needed to relax her face, otherwise she'd get wrinkles.

Kids.

Back to the whole honest to a fault thing.

Sara stopped, eyes gentle. She was intuitive and probably reading too much into that tiny bit of displeasure Dani felt. "Or you can stay and—"

"It's fine." Dani smiled. "I really should get ready for the game."

And great, now there was regret in Sara's eyes.

God, why did she have to be so bad with people?

"Or maybe I could stay for a little?" she asked. "That way I can help you get them over their initial excitement."

Sara smiled again, the regret softening into amusement. "I'm sure you can picture me covered with approximately a hundred palm prints."

Dani's lips twitched. "Maybe."

Sara linked her arm with Dani's. "Come on, we'll use the old table." Thus called because it *was* old, but also because it was stained from years of similar craft projects, crayon marks, and matchbox cars driving over its deep oak finish. "Oh! And I want to introduce you to someone. Roxanne!" She waved her hand, and a slender blond spun to reveal a startlingly beautiful face. Her hair was styled to perfection, soft waves cascading down narrow shoulders, stopping just before gently curved hips. "Come here. I want you to meet Dani. She's the video coach for the team."

Roxanne's hand felt like actual velvet as it brushed Dani's, and she noticed that even Roxanne's nails were perfectly shaped, her nude nail polish impeccable.

They matched the rest of her outfit—crisp jeans with red flats, a shimmery beige and peach floral blouse. She was beautiful and feminine and effortlessly coiffed in a way that Dani knew she never would achieve.

"Hi, Dani," Roxanne said. "It's so nice to meet you. I was actually reading an article about video coaches last week. I didn't realize how much went into it."

"Oh, it's just a job."

Roxanne's brows rose, and Dani realized what that sounded like.

"I mean, I—" She sucked in a breath. "It has good and bad parts, you know. But I really do love it."

"I hear that," Roxanne said with a laugh.

This should have been the point in the conversation where awkward silence descended, but instead, Roxanne asked Dani a few easy questions, mostly about work, which was lucky for the other woman since Dani was most comfortable when talking about programs and editing equipment. Well, lucky was relative, she supposed. Lucky in this case meaning there wasn't awkward silence, but not so lucky as to not have to listen to Dani prattle on.

But during the few minutes they spoke, Roxanne didn't give one indication that she was bored to tears and desperate to escape.

Instead, she asked several intuitive questions.

"I'm a bit of a computer geek," Roxanne said when Dani looked at her with surprise. "I've been spending my spare time building a P.C." God, even her blush was fucking adorable, tiny pink swathes on each cheekbone, as was her self-conscious chuckle. "No wonder I'm single, huh?"

She turned when Aiden ran up to her, wrapped his arms around her waist. "Roxy!"

"Hey, little one," she said, crouching and beginning to speak to him quietly.

"Roxanne works at the gallery," Sara whispered into Dani's

ear as they talked. "I'm going to—*oof!*" Madeline darted over and began begging to see what was in the bag. "Just a second, honey," she told Mandy's daughter. "Yes, it's a craft project that Dani brought."

"Crafts!" Madeline squealed.

Mandy had trailed her daughter across the room, snagging the tote from Sara and laughing. "Yeah, baby." She held up the bag. "The supplies are in here. We just have to go to the old table and get everything set up."

"I've got it," Roxanne said, standing when Aiden ran off again. "I can get things set up so you two can enjoy your chat."

"I—" Dani began.

But without any trace of awkward, Roxanne took Madeline's hand and led her to the table, easily getting everything spread out, even as more kiddos found their way into the supplies. In even movements, her musical voice trailing across the room, her smile bright as the lights inside the arena, she got each kid setup with a plate, a rock, brushes, and paint and didn't even get a speck on her.

Effortless. Again.

So freaking much that Dani should hate her, strictly on principle.

But she couldn't.

Because Roxanne seemed like a really nice person.

"I'll catch you guys later," Mandy said, moving to help Roxanne when a few of the boys thought it was a good idea to chase each other with paintbrushes . . . loaded full of paint.

"I'm going to set her up with Ethan," Sara said quietly.

Scratch that.

She hated Roxanne. She was the worst with her flawless hair and body and smile and no awkward in sight and—

"Isn't she just perfect for him?" Sara said. "I know he's a little scruffy, but he cleans up nice, and they're both just so nice. I can already picture tiny little blond babies with Ethan's gray eyes. They'll be adorable."

Dani's heart twisted and filled with lead, growing heavy, sinking to the bottom of the ocean.

Ocean of despair that was.

The past was weighty, intense, reaching up and sinking its talons deep, reminding her of everything that was wrong with her.

And everything that was right with Roxanne, a woman she hardly knew, and yet a woman she knew would be—

"Dani?"

Perfect.

Beautiful and flawless and *perfect* for Ethan.

The pressure on the seabed compressed her heart, squeezing it on all sides, squashing the organ, forcing out the hope she'd stashed there after her conversation with Ethan.

Wisps flitting away into dark water.

Her heart crumpled smaller and smaller, until she felt nothing.

Nothing except for pain and the urge to clutch her safety net closed.

This was why she didn't let people in.

Because Roxanne was lovely and perfect for Ethan, so much more than Dani could ever hope to be, and her only consolation was that if it hurt this much after a couple of conversations and a near kiss, then she was lucky to have been reminded of it now and not when she was in deeper and—

Fingers on her arm. "Dani?" Sara asked. "Are you okay?"

She shook herself. "S-sorry," she said hurriedly. "I just remembered that I needed to meet with Jess before the game." She edged away from Sara before the other woman could see how deeply the thought of Ethan with anyone else hurt. That was a ridiculous thought. He'd asked her out on one date, and she hadn't even agreed to that much.

He was much better off with a woman like Roxanne than her.

That was just reality.

And if she was in the way, she would deny Ethan his chance at perfect.

She couldn't do that. She . . . *fuck*, but she liked him too much to do that.

Perhaps, if her misery wasn't so heavy and forbidding, perhaps if she wasn't already on that seabed, water and pressure on all sides crushing her, she might have been able to recognize that Ethan could choose to be with who he liked.

Perhaps, if Roxanne just wasn't so freaking perfect, Dani might have seen past the wretchedness that had swept up and was smothering her.

But Roxanne *was* perfect and lovely.

And Dani wasn't good at shrugging off her insecurities.

"I should go," she said.

"Are you sure you're okay?" Sara asked.

A smile, one that felt and probably looked forced. "Just peachy."

Sara's expression darkened. "Are—"

Desperate times called for desperate measures. She patted her pocket, pulled out her cell and glanced at the screen. "Oh, that's Jess, I'd better run."

Sara opened her mouth, protest all over her expression, but Dani put words to action and hustled out the door of the Family Suite. Her face felt hot, and her pulse scattered. God, her lungs weren't working. She couldn't pull in enough air, couldn't breathe.

She jabbed at the elevator button and managed to suck in just enough oxygen to stumble down the hall and into her office.

Then she closed the door, threw the lock, and sank into her chair, thinking how lucky she was to have had this close call.

Otherwise, she might have really gotten hurt.

Yup, she was really lucky.

"Definitely lucky," she whispered.

And if there were tears streaking down her cheeks, then she was just going to ignore them.

God knew, it wasn't the first time.

TWELVE

ETHAN

It took until he got into the locker room and sat down at his cubby before he felt it.

It being Dani's rock, he realized as he reached into his pocket and pulled out the hard object that was jabbing him in the thigh.

Sparks skating down his spine, tiny fireflies floating in his blood as he stroked a finger over the smoothly painted surface. Turquoise flowers and pink toes, glasses sliding down a nose, soft fingers on his jaw.

Want tearing him up inside, need stitching him back together.

God, he was in deep for that woman.

Noise gathered at the door, Coop and Max chatting as they came in, their gazes coming immediately to him, and he knew the gossip train was fully boarded and awaiting departure to its next destination.

As quickly—and slyly—as he could, he stashed the rock in his backpack and set about getting ready for the game.

A quick workout, stretching, copious amounts of foam-rolling, and then finally, at the last possible minute (a fact that used to drive his coaches to worry) getting dressed. But there was a method to his madness. He only got his gear on when he was in the right frame of mind.

Game time.

Or, he thought with an inner snort, *was it game* mind?

Decisions, decisions.

"Someone looks happy," Max said, sitting next to him, literally rocking the boat (bench) with his nosy enthusiasm. "I'm guessing this has to do with a certain shy female, who was looking at you like you're wielding Mjölnir."

Ethan waited for there to be more information in that sentence. When it didn't come, he said, "I think you underestimate my nerdiness."

"Right," Max said. "You're the career student who hasn't had the chance to learn all the important things." A beat. "Like Marvel."

Tugging on his T-shirt, he raised his brows.

"As in one certain blond-haired hero."

More brow-raising.

"As in Thor."

"Ah," he said, loving the irritation and disbelief creeping onto Max's face right now, as if he couldn't believe that someone hadn't heard of Thor and the movies. Ethan knew of both, had watched them, actually, since he did occasionally do something that wasn't book-related, but it was about fucking time that Max got a taste of his own brand of humor (that being mostly annoying and only somewhat funny). "We're talking about Norse mythology now."

Max choked for a moment then recovered. "We're talking about summoning lightning bolts from the sky, kicking ass with a giant hammer, and—" He stopped, probably because Ethan had little to no poker face. "You're fucking with me."

"'Bout time someone does."

Brit.

He glanced up.

She winked. "You boys running with me today?"

"God, no," Ethan said. "I want to have legs for the game."

Brit's pre- and post-game workouts were famous . . . or perhaps infamous was more accurate. She was fast, could run like hell, and no matter how hard Ethan pushed during the workout or trained beforehand, he never could catch up with her. The woman was like liquid lightning, graceful and effortless as she all but flew up and down the steps lining the arena.

"Baby," she grumbled. "Max?"

"Ditto what the Big, Juicy Brain said. Legs. Game. Don't wanna die."

She frowned, sighed heavily. "I miss Stefan. He always ran with me."

"Run with your boyfriend on your own time," Max grumbled. "God knows the man must be glutton for punishment, considering he's the only one who ever comes close to catching you."

Brit blew on her knuckles, buffed them on her shoulder. "That's how he put a ring on it."

Max snorted.

Ethan grinned, just as Coop and Blue strolled up, workout gear on. Those two, apparently, were gluttons for punishment.

"Ready?" Coop asked.

"These two"—Brit waved a hand at the pair—"are real men." Her voice rose. "Just in case anyone was looking for them." Boos and hisses abounded, along with a few rolled-up socks tossed in her direction. Which she caught effortlessly because she had that killer glove hand. "Later, losers," she called, throwing them back.

Ethan grinned, shook his head, and got ready for the game.

His way.

Though he found himself adding one new ritual.

Brushing his thumb over the rock Dani had painted and remembering the feel of strawberry-scented skin.

Yeah, life was good.

———

The game went great.

One of those perfect matchups where the system worked, bounces went their way, and they won handily in front of a kick-ass home crowd.

He'd skated hard, done his job, coming off the ice on a high that would take several hours to come down from.

Of course, he had one thought of how he'd like to come down.

Or . . . with whom, anyway.

Maybe he could tempt Dani into a milkshake from the Dairy. He wouldn't call it a date . . . just an exchange of milk-based fluids? He froze, hands in his hair, shampoo running down his back. Yeah, no, he wouldn't sell it that way. Instead, he'd call it . . . a chance to discuss the positive qualities of rock-painting in correlation to reduced stress and increased satisfaction? This time he snorted because that, too, was horrible.

How about just going for milkshakes in a no pressure, no expectation, no—

Just milkshakes.

Keep it simple.

Satisfied with that, Ethan knew he'd even slum it with a frozen yogurt variety (on the diet plan), if it meant that he could chisel out some time with Dani.

She was shy, nervous around people in general, but sometimes she relaxed with him, and seeing that smile, hearing her talk without being self-conscious . . . well, the glimpses he'd gotten of that side of her made him feel like a fucking superhero.

Not to mention the little moan she'd given, rasping up from the back of her throat, sliding through the air and caressing his skin like velvet.

That made him feel like a superhero who was desperate to kiss every inch of her.

And then to plunge deep inside, to get his hands on that lush ass, to hold her close and bring them both up to and over the edge again and again and again.

But first, he'd start with milkshakes.

Because if he continued down this train of thinking, he'd end up giving himself a boner. In the locker room. With no shortage of teammates to tease him for eternity about it.

Shuddering, he pushed the thoughts from his mind and took his time through his post-game routine, knowing that Dani would have plenty of work to keep her busy in the meantime, then he dressed and slipped out into the hall, finding himself— look at that—in front of her office.

The door was open, Jess, her assistant, was shrugging into her jacket and gathering up her purse.

Their voices—one laced with humor and plenty of volume (Jess) and the other softer, more melodic (Dani)—tangled in the air, weaving together into a pleasant series of techie terms and players' names. Then Jess called out a goodbye and slipped into the hall, nearly stumbling into him.

"Oh," she murmured. "I'm sorry, I—"

"It's okay," he said. "My fault."

She looked up at him, and he struggled to keep his focus on her, his gaze already drifting to the office, to Dani.

"Go easy on her," Jess whispered. "She's had a rough day of it."

He frowned, wondered what that meant. Dani had been smiling when he'd left her, and not a fake one either, the beautiful, genuine smile he was just starting to learn. So, what had happened in the last few hours?

Nodding as he puzzled that out, he waited until Jess had disappeared around the corner before knocking lightly on the doorjamb.

Striking brown eyes on his.

Eyes that filled with happiness for one glorious heartbeat before they went cold.

And God, cold was such a fucking lame word to describe the

ice that overlaid Dani's gaze, that shut down her expression, that had her shoulders curving forward and down, just slightly.

Just enough that he knew something bad had happened.

A vice clenching around his heart, frost prickling through his veins sharp enough to make his fingertips ache, he stepped inside, closing—and locking—the door, for good measure. "What happened?" he asked without preamble.

She became a statue.

Like one of those iron ones outside the library, a still life in repose, a granite formed into an amalgamation of life. But the statues didn't have her pain.

Pain that was sharp enough to wound.

"What is it?" he asked, crossing over to her. "Is someone hurt?"

In an instant her face changed, going completely blank, shoulders straightening, chin tilting up. She would have appeared . . . well, not completely at ease so much as neutral and unaffected—if he hadn't seen her in agony just seconds before.

"Nope." The P made a popping sound, and he was processing that serrated noise as she turned back to her computer, effectively giving him the cold shoulder.

"Dani?"

"You should go."

He gripped the back of her chair, spun it to face him. "What's going on, sweetheart?"

Silence, those russet and amber eyes on his then away then on his again. "I'm not going to date you."

Well, fuck, there went milkshake night.

He crouched down, hesitated for a second, then placed his hands on her jean-covered knees. "I'm going to ask one more time. What happened?"

The barest hint of ice retreated.

"Nothing's happened," she said. "The cost-benefit ratio of having a relationship with someone I work with is too great. I'm not doing it."

The cost-benefit ratio?

Seriously?

His fingers tightened. "Dani."

She stood, and he rocked back to his heels for a brief moment before he regained his balance and found his feet. "Look, you're fun to talk to. You even make me laugh every once in a while. But I'm not the person for you, and I never will be." She opened the door. "Now, go."

That was utter horseshit. She was herself, and that was enough for him. He opened his mouth to tell her just that.

"Th—"

Fanny walked up. "Dani, you ready to go—" She stopped, realizing several moments too late that the office wasn't empty. Her gaze moved from him to Dani. "Or I could just come back . . . *later?*"

"No," Dani said sharply. "Ethan was just leaving."

He met her eyes for a heartbeat, but it was long enough for him to recognize that he needed to regroup. In that moment, he wasn't going to be able to convince her of anything, least of all to tell him what was really going on. Fucking hell, what had happened?

Fanny's brows were lifted, but she slid back a pace, as though she were going to be the one leaving.

He glanced at Dani. "We'll talk later."

"No," she said, with a streak of fierce determination. "We won't."

His temper spiked, something that Ethan usually controlled, and for an instant, he considered hauling Dani against his chest and giving her the kiss he should have laid on her earlier. It would be good, he knew that.

He'd actually taken a step toward her before he realized what he was doing and stopped, clenching his hands into fists and shoving them down to his sides. He could kiss her, could make her like it.

But . . . fucking hell, he also knew that she deserved their first kiss to be something of passion and need rather than anger.

Fanny's voice intruded on that haze of fury. "I'll just—"

"No," he snapped then forced himself to soften his tone. "I'm sorry," he said. "I'm gone. Enjoy your . . ." His eyes drifted to Dani, to the muscle clenching in her jaw, her knuckles pressed in sharp relief against her skin. For as much as she wasn't talking, he knew this was about something deep, deeper than he could get out of her in just a few moments. He needed to regroup. ". . . evening."

And then with one more look at the woman who'd shyly woven her way into his heart, he turned and walked away.

Thirteen

"Want to tell me what that was about?" Fanny asked.

Hell fucking no.

She wasn't going to tell *anyone* about what had happened in the Family Suite. Not because she felt ashamed of the way she'd reacted—which, okay, yes, she *did* feel ashamed because she hated that she was still a person who didn't value herself. She should be like the other women of the Gold—strong and confident and woke and . . . lots of other things. Equality for all, including the shy, dorky girls. Confidence for days.

She should have just told Sara that she wasn't going to set Roxanne up with Ethan.

Because he was hers.

Except . . . he *wasn't* hers.

And why would he want to be with someone like her?

"Ugh," she groaned, plunking her head onto her desk and then *thunking* it several times for good measure. "I." *Thump.* "Don't." *Thump.* "Know." *Thump.* "What." *Thump.* "I'm." *Thump.* "Doing." *Thump*—

Or it would have been another thump, if Fanny hadn't caught her shoulder and tugged her up.

"The team needs that brain," she said.

Misery coursed through Dani. "I—um—I—"

"Easy on the wheels zipping around in there"—a tap to Dani's temple—"I swear, smoke's gonna start pouring out of your ears pretty soon."

She shut her eyes. "I'm a mess, Fanny. I can't even agree to go on one date without freaking out."

Her friend squeezed her shoulder. "Let's go get a drink."

Dani's lids peeled back. "You're not going to pump me for information?"

Fanny straightened, leaned a hip against her desk. "Honestly?" A pause, gaze on her until she nodded. "You don't look like you can handle an inquisition, bub. Let's just get ourselves good and drunk, eat too many carbs, and then you can figure it out tomorrow, okay?"

Surprise and relief warred with that ever-present anxiety and self-doubt. "You'd do that?"

People weren't nice to her—

Except, she couldn't use that excuse anymore, could she?

Because without thinking hard, she could come up with a list that was plenty long of people who were nice to her, people who cared—and they weren't just her family, not any longer.

She had Fanny and Jess. Sara and Brit and both Rebeccas and—

The point was that she was living her life like it was the past, instead of realizing she was a thirty-year-old woman who wasn't on the receiving end of a bunch of mean-ass kids.

And it was high time she stopped giving that past power.

"Dani?" A shake of her shoulder. "Booze. Carbs. Sleep. Okay?"

Since that was better than living in her own head, letting it twist around her like barbed wire, hurting whether she moved or not, but doubly so when she moved, Dani pushed up from her seat and nodded. "That sounds good."

Fanny smiled, laced her arm with Dani's. "Great. I'll drive."

"But—"

"We'll have a slumber party at my place, but we'll stop by yours first, get your stuff packed for the road trip. That way in the morning, we can grab brekkie at Molly's and come straight here to hop on the bus."

Dani's brows drew together because there was a lot to process in that. Starting with, "But you don't travel with the team."

"I'm hitching a ride," she said. "My family is coming to the game in Chicago, and then we're road-tripping it for a week."

"That sounds fun."

"You haven't driven with my mother." A grin. "I'll be lucky to come back in one piece."

Dani found herself laughing.

Somehow, after she'd spent the last hours in a perpetual cycle of self-flagellation, she was laughing and walking arm-in-arm with her friend, and the bottom wasn't falling out of the world, and . . . she was beginning to wonder if she hadn't been the least bit hasty with Ethan.

Cue more internal whipping.

"Dani? Is there a reason you look like you've swallowed a lemon?"

"I'm . . ." She sighed. "My head is a mess."

"And here I've promised to not give you an inquisition."

Dani snorted. "You'd take advantage of a woman on the edge?"

"Hell yes, I would." A beat, a squeeze of her arm. "But I won't because I promised."

"A woman who sticks by her word."

"Yeah." Fanny nudged Dani with her elbow. "Kind of like my friend."

"I haven't had that many friends," she whispered, the words slipping off her tongue uninvited.

Fanny tugged her to a stop. "And why's that, do you think?"

"Because I'm . . ."

A nerd, shy, self-conscious . . . not worthy.

The last crept through her mind like insidious ivy crawling up the trunk of a tree. She waited, expecting the pang that usually accompanied the thought, the cold frost that followed, creeping in through the fronts of her sneakers, soaking into her socks, chilling her toes.

But the pang, the iciness didn't come.

Instead, something red-hot flared in its place, and suddenly, her brain went clear. She wasn't what they had said.

And why, why had it taken her so long to see?

"I was . . . well, for a long time I've made myself small."

Fanny's expression gentled. "Why, babe? When you're so fucking big and bright?"

"Because I'm an idiot?"

A shake of her head, brown locks flailing behind her. "Nope. That's one thing you're not."

A sigh. "Because I'm scared?"

Fanny tapped her nose. "Ding. Ding. Give the girl a prize."

Laughter floated up, like a balloon drifting toward the sky, escaping her lips in a quiet puff of sound. "I thought you said no inquisitions?"

"Well, you gave me a freebie, what's a girl supposed to do?"

"I—"

The question was what was *she* supposed to do? Because seriously, what the fuck was she doing? She needed to find Ethan and explain, to tell him . . . *something* that would come to her, knowing coming to fruition as she went after him.

It was bad. She needed to—

"Hang on." She tugged her arm free, started down the hall. "I need to—"

"Hey!"

She stopped, turned around.

Fanny's mouth was tipped up at the corners. "Should I wait?"

Nerves bubbled into the space laughter had just occupied. But . . . fuck . . . hadn't she been scared long enough?

Yes. *Yes.*

"No," she told Fanny. "Don't wait."

"Carbs and booze another night!"

She nodded in agreement . . . and then she ran in a very undignified manner toward the parking lot.

When she burst out through the door, the air was cold, spreading across her face, tightening her skin, drying out her lips —or maybe that was nerves. Because the urge to spin back around and run inside to find Fanny for the booze with a side of carbs was intense.

Grew even more intense when she found Ethan standing there, his gaze on the ground, his hands fisted at his sides.

Turn tail.

Run.

Hide.

Her spine prickled, her foot slid back.

And then his stare drifted up, collided with hers.

She couldn't miss the hurt in his eyes, the misery, the despair. The trifecta of emotions was a literal gut punch, and her foot stopped its motion. Then moved forward to join the other.

Her throat seized.

Words exploded.

"Sara brought a beautiful woman named Roxanne to set you up with, and I freaked out. I thought that I couldn't possibly measure up and shouldn't get in the way of someone who clearly fit you better than me."

His face turned . . . scary. That was the only way she could think to describe it, but instead of stoppering the words up, it only made them come faster.

"And I've always been quiet. My family is great, but they're all big personalities, and it was just easier to blend into the background, to sit back and enjoy the show. I wasn't ever the type of girl who'd battle to be in the front. I was just happy with what I had."

A fierce expression.

Gentle fingers lifting to grasp hers, his thumb brushing the inside of her wrist, tracing light circles on her skin.

And she found that the rest of it wasn't so hard.

"Then I reached for more," she whispered. "Then I dared to want something big and beautiful, and . . . the universe slapped me back." Her eyes closed, and those fingers gripped tighter, tugging her away from the door, slipping an arm around her waist and bringing her body flush against the side of his.

Warm and strong, one hand wiping away the tears she hadn't even known escaped, then drawing her even closer as voices came close.

"You coming, Eth?" Brit called from somewhere nearby.

Ethan shifted her, shielding her body with his, and she felt a piece of her heart chip away, slip right through the holes in her safety net and drift over to him, to his palm, to those gentle circles on her skin. "Another time," he called.

"Okay. But just so you know," she called back, "I'm pretending I don't see Dani with you."

"Stay in your lane, Brit."

"That's for race car drivers."

A sigh. "Then between the pipes."

"That I can do," she hollered. "See ya."

Then she was gone, and Dani was alone with Ethan again, only this time they weren't standing in the shadows next to the arena, they were moving.

Or maybe they'd been moving the whole time.

Because by the time she processed they were walking, Ethan was beeping the locks on his car, opening the door. "Sit," he murmured, plunking her into the passenger's seat and reaching over her to buckle her belt.

Then he crossed around the front of the car, got in, and drove out of the parking lot.

He didn't speak as he drove, navigating the bright lights of the waterfront, the semi-quiet streets. There were always a few people out in a city like San Francisco, but this late, it was a muted hum of activities, the traffic gone, most people tucked safely into their beds. She turned to look out at the water, wanting to explain more, wanting to apologize, to find something to make him understand.

Ethan reached out and squeezed her knee. "It's okay."

"That I freaked out or I can't find the words to explain?"

Another squeeze. "Both. You don't owe me anything, sweetheart. Explanation or words or otherwise."

"But . . ."

When she trailed off, words lost again, he didn't get impatient, just waited.

"I want to give it to you."

His fingers convulsed.

She sucked in a breath.

He turned into a parking lot, the lights twinkling at regular intervals, the water of the Bay in the distance. It was a clear night, the moon shining down on the waves and their crests, turning them shades of black and gray and silver. But the beauty of that undulating mix of salt and water couldn't hold her attention.

Not when every cell in her body was focused on the man next to her.

Not when he said, "I only want what you're willing to give."

And that unlocked the rest of it.

"I fell for the popular boy in high school." The memories threatened to swell up, to overwhelm her, but she shoved them down. "The long and short is that I was the baby in my family, the quiet one, the protected one, and I fell for a boy who didn't believe in protecting me in any sense. I was too weak or infatuated or *stupid* to recognize what was happening, and by the time I did, I was pregnant."

Ethan sucked in a breath.

"It's stupid, really," she said, hating the sharp slice of pain, the way this truth made her want to curl up and go quiet, to lock the hurt down. "I figured we'd get married, and everything would be perfect. I'd somehow have the fairy tale ending."

Her heart thudded.

Her palms were sweaty.

Her throat was tight.

But Ethan didn't rush her.

And she found that her heart slowed, her throat loosened, and the moisture on her palms dried.

"He just . . . pretended I didn't exist." A breath. "I told him I was pregnant, and he just dropped me off at my house, and then at school the next day, he ignored me completely. It wasn't even hours before he was with the most popular girl in school." A tall, slender blond, much like Roxanne. Except, she'd been snake-mean where Roxanne seemed nice.

"I was a teenager. I was emotional and heartbroken and hurt and—" A shake of her head. "And I tried to talk to him, but he was . . . well, cruel. So, then I knew I couldn't rely on him, couldn't expect a happy ending from him, so I thought the baby and I would make our own." Her eyes burned at the memory. "But I lost the baby, and I got really sick."

His fingers were like a vise on her leg, but instead of hurting, they grounded her, helped her finish the story.

"My parents hadn't known until I started bleeding, until it was bad, and they needed to call an ambulance." She shook her head, a thousand little slices of agony crisscrossing through her insides. "I was in the hospital for a while, and after I recovered, my family . . . they gave me a pass. I homeschooled for the rest of the school year, and we moved the next. New school. Fresh start for my senior year," she said with a sigh. "But I was different, smaller. Quieter. No happy ending. No fairy tale. No prince. No boyfriend."

Dani shuddered out a breath.

There it was. Her whole sad sob story.

One no one knew except her family.

But . . . shouldn't this feel better? To get everything off her chest? Cutting the bindings, releasing their hold on her?

Instead, the past was like a mace inside her, spikes jabbing at her from all sides, her spine as rigid and stiff as a piece of wood. God this *hurt,* and she wanted to crawl back into herself, to cover the pain, the spikes, wrap up and bury the splinters from that wood.

She wanted to be small again.

She wanted to not *feel* again.

No sooner had that thought crossed her mind before Ethan moved.

The car jerked as he shoved his seat back and then in the next instant, her seat belt was unlatched and she was hauled over the console, plunked into his lap with his warm, strong arms wrapped tight around her.

"I'm sorry."

Just two words but filled with empathy instead of pity for the first time. Her family had been sympathetic, sure, but they'd largely been pitying. Poor Dani. Poor, naïve, unworldly Dani.

It was different with Ethan, however.

No pity.

No pat on the head.

Just warm arms and a steady heartbeat against her ear when he brought her even closer.

"I should be over this by now." She found the words she'd thought to herself a million times before allowing them to slip out, and his arms grew tighter. "I was a teenager, and it was puppy love, and—"

"You were hurt and lost a dream. That doesn't just go away." A soft hand on her back, rubbing lightly. "That changes a person. Irrevocably."

"And what about your dreams?" she whispered, lifting up, her eyes meeting his. "Which ones have you lost?"

A shadow of pain across his face, and guilt swarmed her.

"I'm sorry," she whispered. "I didn't mean. I—"

"It's okay," he said, just as quietly. "I lost a friend. First year in the league. He was struck and killed by a drunk driver."

"Oh, Ethan." She covered his jaw with her palm. "I'm so sorry."

She half-expected him to say something along the lines of life happens or shit gets real or bad things sometimes happen to good people, or one of a myriad of other platitudes people pitch to each other when they don't know what to say or how to react.

Instead, he covered her hand with his own, his gaze on hers. "Thank you."

The moment stretched, growing taut, expectation coursing through the air, and then his lips brushed her forehead, her cheek, her jaw . . . her lips.

It was sparks, not like she'd expected after the hall, after the door.

Rather, it was sunshine on the tip of her nose on a summer's day, heat caressing her collarbones, her shoulders, drifting down to her fingers.

Gentle and so fucking sweet that it made her eyes prickle.

Then his tongue touched the seam of her mouth. Her lips parted, and that warmth exploded into heat. His beard was roughened velvet against her skin, the most intoxicating abrasion of her life, and his tongue, when it stroked along hers, was a sleek, hot dart driving pleasure to follow in the wake of that heat. Her fingers wove into his hair, the soft locks like silk on her palms, needing him even nearer.

Even as the thought entered her mind, Ethan's hands were on her waist, pulling her closer, his cock hard against her center, sparking through her nerves, sending pleasure coursing through her, despite the layers between them.

One hand slid up her side, and she groaned as those sparks spread, coalescing into a kind of need she'd never felt before.

And just as it was getting *really* good, just as it was burning so fucking incredibly and she found herself almost completely undone, Ethan pulled back.

"You are so fucking strong."

The rest of her heart shattered into a million pieces, those shards floating through the air and reforming . . . to encompass him.

She stretched up and kissed him again.

Fourteen

He was hard and aching, furious and in agony that Dani had been hurt, and he couldn't do a damned thing about it.

But nothing eclipsed the feeling of the key turning in the lock, of the sudden pop of a door opening, of right.

This was right.

This was *everything*.

She pushed at his chest, tearing her mouth from his. He almost expected her to draw back, to retreat, but instead she stayed close, her forehead resting on his, her palm on his shoulder.

A tear dropped onto his shirt.

Shit.

"Did I—?"

She pressed her finger to his mouth. "Why is it so easy with you?"

"Because this is right."

Her lips parted, her breath hitching, and he shifted, leaning forward to kiss her again, needing to kiss her.

It was a directive written into his DNA.

She slid her tongue into his mouth, tangling it with his. Desire pooled in his stomach, pressing his cock even more firmly against the zipper of his slacks. He really fucking hated himself for not having taken her directly back to his house. If he had, they wouldn't be having this conversation in a car, wouldn't be crammed in between the seat and the steering wheel, when it really would have been much better if they'd been horizontal—

"Why," she asked, pulling back again, her hand resting on his chest, probably feeling the way it was pounding haphazard and totally out of control, "do you taste so fucking good?"

He groaned, rested his palm on her nape. "Because this is right," he said again.

And as much as he wanted to kiss her again, to get lost in her taste and the feel of her body, he gently set her away from him, sliding her over into her own seat, sucking in a breath when she shakily pressed her fingers to her lips.

He wanted to kiss her again, to have her back in his arms.

But they were in an empty parking lot in the city, and it was after midnight, and he needed to keep her safe.

"Can I drive you home?"

Glazed eyes met his.

"I'll pick you up in the morning, and we can have breakfast."

"Or," she whispered, "maybe you could stay?"

His cock somehow grew harder, and he nearly reached over the console and grabbed her again. Instead, however, he cupped her cheek, told her the truth. "I want that," he whispered. "I've fantasized about that in six thousand different ways, but . . ." He trailed off at the disappointment on her face, and for a moment he wondered why he was being a Cub Scout, but then the answer was easy. She was important. She *meant* something. So, that's why he'd drive her home, kiss her goodnight on the porch, and continue winning her trust.

Her face evened out, the warmth tucked back into cool. "You have the game tomorrow. You'll need your rest."

"No." He turned on the car, navigated out of the lot. "I don't give a shit about rest. I give a shit about you, and I don't want you to do something that you might—" He couldn't force out the word regret. "I don't want to move too fast. I like you, Dani, more than I probably should, considering I've been fantasizing about you longer than I've actually spoken to you."

He heard her inhale.

"So, I'm going to drive you home where I'm going to make out with you on your front porch, and then I'm going to see your sweet ass in the morning, so I can buy you a breakfast I can drool over but can't actually eat myself." He glanced over, saw her lips quirk then looked back at the road. "I'll choke down my oatmeal and fruit, my single allotted cup of coffee, and then I'll drive us to the rink where we'll get on a plane, and know what?"

"What?"

He winked at her. "I promise to save the seat next to me."

She laughed.

"Now," he said, getting onto the freeway and heading south. "Tell me, how far have you gotten through that stack of books from the library?"

Silence.

Then she laughed. "How far do you think?"

He met her eyes for a heartbeat before returning his focus in front of him. "Pretty damned far, I think."

"You'd be right."

Another glance. "Will you tell me about your favorite?"

"Favorite book? Or favorite from that stack?"

"What? Do I look stupid? Favorite from the stack," he teased. "It's impossible for a true bookworm to choose her favorite."

"Spoken by a true bookworm?"

"My favorite that I've read recently was a list-topping thriller. Even though it was a bit formulaic, it was a nice reprieve from scientific papers." A beat, another brief look toward her. "Now, show me yours."

Laughter filled the car, and it was the best fucking thing he'd heard in a long time.

They talked about books as he drove.

Then he got his kiss. Well, *kisses*.

And then he went back to his place, jerked off because he had the erection to end all erections, and even as he slept, his mind was only on one thing.

Dani.

The taste of her. The feel of her. The sound of her laughter filling the air.

———

"And then Blue tried to steal Max's figurines," Dani said, "but Anna found out, and she thought it was stupid as hell and was really, *really* done with them pranking each other, so instead she stole Blue's lucky socks."

He scooped up a bite of his oatmeal. "Okay, so this is the part I've heard. Or at least the part that had Blue tearing apart the locker room looking for those damned socks."

Dani laughed. "Poor guy."

A shrug, his lips twitching. "He was in full meltdown mode. You don't get between hockey players and their good luck charms."

"Well, from what I heard, no harm was done, and Max *and* Blue figured it out."

"They certainly did." A beat, his lips twitching. "Eventually."

Because with a little help from Angie, Anna had also stolen Max's special lucky figurine he had to stroke before every game—which sounded grosser than it was in actuality—then had left a ransom note for both the socks and the figurine, forcing Max and Blue to work together to rescue those good luck charms.

"So, the socks and figurine were found," Dani said, scooping up a bite of what looked to be a truly delicious waffle. "And the prank war was over."

"And we all breathed a sigh of relief in the locker room."

A giggle as she ate more of her waffle. "How long did it take for the dubious duo to find them?"

"Too close to game time, as far as Bernard was concerned." Ethan chuckled. "Far too soon, as far as the guys in the room went."

"That's a shame."

"Eh." He scraped the last bit of his oatmeal up. "It was a fantastic prank on Anna and Angie's parts."

"Angie told me Max made her sleep on the couch."

Ethan choked.

Dani giggled again. "But that she woke up in Max's arms."

Ethan set his spoon down, smiled. That sounded much more like his friend and teammate. "Those women keep their men on their toes."

"Still want to date me?" Amber and russet eyes glimmered with mirth, but there was also a layer of insecurity beneath.

"I'm looking forward to tiptoeing all over the place."

Her expression shifted, warmed. "Last chance."

He reached across the table, took her hand. "Scared?"

"Fucking terrified." Her shoulders rose and fell on an exhale. "But I'm also ready to finally live my life."

His fingers twitched. "What should we do first?"

"First, we should pay the bill." A smile. "Then we should get our butts to the rink so we don't miss the bus."

He glanced at his watch then reached to pull out his wallet. "I'm loving this whole dating thing already."

"Then you're going to love that I already paid the bill, so we can just go straight out to your car."

"What?" His brows drew together, his hand still half in his pocket, since he'd been in the process of pulling out his wallet. "What do you mean—" But his question was cut off when Dani sat down next to him, tugging his hand out of the opening, shoving his wallet back inside.

"I said, I got it." Her fingers lightly brushed his. "Which means you still owe me a date."

Joy swirled through him, a tiny tornado growing in intensity with each second he spent in the presence of this woman. "I'll take that deal," he said, sliding his hand up her arm, lightly gripping the side of her neck. "Because it means more time with you."

"I like you, Ethan Korhonen."

"Well, right back at you, Dani Eastbrooke."

He brushed his lips over hers.

She turned the kiss into something that had his heart pounding, his cock going to granite.

Then she stood, took his hand, and he knew he was in for a hell of a ride.

Fifteen

She was sitting up front by Fanny; the man who made every cell in her body sit up and pay attention was several rows back.

She'd been intending to sit by him, but then Max had gotten ahold of Ethan, and Fanny had come to carry out her aforementioned interrogation, and . . . next thing she knew, she was in her normal row on the bus, her friend chatting her ear off as the vehicle got loaded.

Brit walked by, winking when she caught Dani's gaze as she made her way to the back of the bus.

Seniority ruled when it came to seat position.

Coaches up front, then support staff, then rookies on back to the senior citizens.

Dani wondered what Brit might say if the goalie knew that Dani mentally referred to her, Blane, and Max as the senior citizens.

They *were* the oldest players.

But the lithe, strong Brit wouldn't be happy.

Still, Dani filed it away for use at a future date—maybe

during one of those times where she was hanging with the women of the Gold and worked up the courage to actually say something.

If she were living her life for real now, she'd need a few teasing statements stowed away and ready to roll.

"What are you smiling about?"

She blinked, glanced up to see that Fanny had vacated her seat, and it was suddenly occupied by a man who took up much more space than her tiny figure-skating friend. "I was categorizing Brit as a senior citizen."

He froze. His face an expression in shock.

And then he burst out laughing, drawing the notice of pretty much everyone on the bus. They were probably wondering what the heck quiet, shy Dani could be saying to make a man like Ethan laugh so riotously.

But for the first time ever in her life, Dani didn't care what anyone else was thinking.

She only cared what Ethan was thinking, and she supposed, what *she* was thinking. And the thoughts floating through her mind were light, happy ones, cautious optimism and a need to know everything about this man. His family, his parents, every sad and positive story of his life.

She wanted to know his favorite color and food and—

"Why's there smoke coming out of your ears?"

"What's your favorite color?"

He straightened, lips parting and then curving. "It's like that, huh?"

"It's a perfectly acceptable first date question."

"We're on a date?"

Her sigh was disgruntled, and she swatted at his chest. "We're going to be at some point. Well, if you stop being such a pain in my ass, that is."

He grinned, his gray eyes dancing, and she nudged him with her elbow. Which just had him snagging her arm, tucking it against him . . . tugging *her* against him. Her breath caught, desire swirling through her, and she was quite desperate to taste him again.

His hand came to her cheek, his thumb brushing along her bottom lip. He groaned. "Don't look at me like that."

She would give almost anything right then to be able to kiss him like she had on her porch the night before, like her body was an extension of his and if she just kept sipping at his mouth, the rest of the world could go on without them.

"Not helping," he murmured, that thumb still running back and forth.

"You came up to sit by me."

"I like you," he said. "I like to sit by people I like."

"That's a lot of likes."

He tapped her nose. "Sass. I like that, too."

She laughed, shook her head, leaning back enough so she could focus. "Well then, just answer the question already. I want to know *all* the little things."

"*All* the little things?"

"Leave the comedy to Max."

"Fuck."

She froze at the suddenly gruff tone. "What?"

"I really fucking like you, Eastbrooke."

This whole conversation, paired with his body next to hers, was threatening to turn her into a pile of mush. Which meant that she needed to pull herself together. Otherwise there would just be a pile of Gold emblazoned clothing on the floor sitting in a Dani puddle. "All right. All right," she said. "Enough of that." She waved a hand. "I'm ordering you to answer my first date question."

He paused. "I think I like taking orders from you."

"*I* think I can't give you the kind of orders I really want, so you need to behave yourself for the duration of the ride to the airport."

Warm fingers laced through hers, a rough palm engulfing her hand, tendrils of heat curling up her arm, sliding through her middle, and his eyes were filled with liquid lightning when they came to hers and held, the air between them crackling. "Raincheck on the orders, love."

Her lips parted, her lungs shuddering. "Be good."

"As long as you promise to stroke me at some point in the future."

The heat was no longer a curl. It was an inferno, a forest fire, a volcano exploding within her. She swallowed hard. "Ethan," she whispered.

"Raincheck, sweetheart."

"Your fault," she murmured.

His smile was sexy and scorching and just the right kind of wicked. "Definitely my fault." Then he straightened, pulling slightly away from her, the fog of his nearness dissipating, allowing her to at least put a few thoughts together.

"Favorite color. STAT."

"Blue," he stated without preamble. Then paused, said, "Actually, no. Not just blue. Turquoise."

And out of his pocket, he produced the stone she'd slipped him the night before.

Her heart was a kitten in her chest, batting a ball of yarn around inside her torso, twisting this way and that.

"Yours?" he murmured, sliding closer as Coop made his way down the aisle. Calle had slid into the row in front of them, and Dani didn't miss the look she tossed their way.

Gossip would be flying.

Or *was* flying already.

She could feel the gazes on them.

A tug of her hair as the bus started moving forward. She blinked, reprocessed the conversation. "Yellow," she whispered.

"Why?" he asked.

"Why?" she repeated.

"Yeah." His thigh pressed to hers. "Why is yellow your favorite color?"

"It's bright." A shrug. "Like sunshine and warm sand and pineapple juice."

He leaned close, his lips coming to her ear. "Did you just call warm sand yellow?"

She was focused on Ethan, on his lips brushing the lobe of her ear, on the goose bumps his warm breath raised on her skin, on the heat from his body, so his words didn't immediately process.

Then they did.

Straightening, she looked down her nose at him. "Really?"

He leaned in, nipped her bottom lip. "Really. It's a travesty. Clearly, sand is beige, not yellow."

"You have permission to smack him," Calle said, glancing over her shoulder with a smirk. "No man should be that at ease when he's trying to win over a woman he likes."

Ethan bent in again. "For the record, I'm not at *ease*." His eyes flicked down, drawing hers to follow, to see that he was hard in his slacks.

"Oh," she murmured, biting her lip.

"But I *am* trying to win over the woman I like," he said. "Now, it's my turn to ask some First Date questions, okay?"

Her heart stuttered, that kitty with its ball of yarn making a reappearance, as the bus pulled onto the freeway, as Ethan began peppering her with more First Date questions. Which she was fine with answering, so long as she was able to get his answers in return. She nodded, whispered, "Okay."

He smiled.

She smiled.

And by the time they got on the plane, she'd learned his favorite TV show, food, place he'd traveled, animal, and superhero movie—*The Office,* steak, New Zealand, lion, and *Captain America: Civil War.* She'd approved of all his choices, aside from the steak, as clearly a Caesar salad was the best food on the planet, and while she liked all the Marvel movies, her favorite supe flick was *Wonder Woman* (the first, clearly . . . because that thigh jiggle and Chris Pine and former princesses being badass warrior queens).

They kept talking as they pulled their respective supplies out —laptop for her, pens, notebooks, and reference materials for him —and then, somehow, effortlessly they fell into silence, working side-by-side without a weird transition of quiet. The conversation just stilled, they both worked until they got drowsy—or at least, she did, closing her laptop after a few hours because planes always made her sleepy.

And then Ethan did an amazing thing.

Without a word, or even seeming to look at her, he lifted the armrest, wrapped an arm around her, and then coaxed her to lie down in his lap, her head on his thigh, her shoulder pressed to his leg, his fingers stroking lightly through her hair.

Her eyes slid closed.

The rumble of the engines coaxed her under.

She was out in moments.

Sixteen

Ethan

"Hey," he murmured.

For once, Dani didn't jump.

She just spun in her chair and stood, crossing over to him with a smile that made him feel as though he could lasso the sun. "That was some move tonight, Korhonen."

He wrapped his arms around her waist. "Want to come somewhere with me?"

They were off the next day and would fly out the following evening. Tonight, however, they were in Denver, it was beautiful, and he had the need to take Dani on their first official date.

She smiled. "Yeah, I do." She spun, packed up her equipment and shoved it into her backpack, which she swung up onto her shoulder.

Which he promptly snagged back down her shoulder and then lifted up onto his.

"You just played," she began. "You're tired—"

"I'm a man."

Her brows lifted. "And that means what exactly? That I can't carry my own bags?"

"Sass." He tapped her nose. "No," he said. "It just means that you don't need to, whether they're filled with rocks and paint or computer equipment."

"And what can I do with my *womanly*, delicate arms?"

God, that arch tone brought forth his naughty librarian fantasies.

"Wait," she said, interrupting him before he could answer that, which was probably for the best because he didn't have a good answer for her question anyway.

However, when she continued talking, he realized he was in even more trouble.

"Why are you blushing?" She snagged his hand when he tried to turn for the door. "What's with the red cheeks, Korhonen?"

Dani in a short skirt and knee highs, telling him she'd check the reference stack for him, that was the cause for his red cheeks.

Also because in his fantasy, that reference stack would be on the bottom shelf.

Bending over, a glimpse of a lush ass. He'd hop the counter, lift her skirt, and—he cursed under his breath when his cock went hard.

Romance, not fucking.

Romance.

Not *fucking*.

He swallowed hard. "Just a post-game flush," he said.

Her brows went up, and he knew she didn't buy that for one second.

Which was why he slid his arm around her waist, tugged her against him, and kissed her. It wasn't gentle or careful. It was a touch borne of need and fantasy, of that moment of dreaming about something for so long, thinking it would never come, even while wishing so fucking desperately that it would.

Sensation roiling through his skin, sparking down from lips to toes. She tasted sweet and spicy, as though she'd just had a stick of cinnamon gum but coated her lips in frosting.

Strawberry frosting.

Her tongue dipped into his mouth, fanning the flames of that spice, draping it across his taste buds, boiling the cytoplasm in his cells, heating his DNA and changing it, transforming it, *morphing* it into something that didn't just exist to perpetuate his own survival, not any longer. Instead, it existed for her, for Dani, for this intoxicating, lovely woman who was quiet, but not with him. Who held her painful memories tight, but shared so he could understand. Who didn't let very many people in, but had let him in.

Her nape was soft against his palm, her curls bouncing when she came closer, when she tilted her head back, tickling the skin of his hand, and the quiet moan, the rasp of his name transmitting from her mouth to his had him fighting the urge to strip her naked and kiss every inch of her.

Work.

They were at work.

Slowly, he wrestled with his control, first finding a slender thread buried deep, gradually drawing it forth, coiling it as he struggled to find another, and then another. Until he had a good-sized chunk of it, until he was able to slow the kiss, to lift his mouth.

His hands . . . he hadn't yet found the control to remove them from her body.

But she didn't seem to mind, not with every lush inch of her pressed to his front—which wasn't exactly helping him in his quest to remove his hands. Still, the way she stared up at him, pupils dilated, lips swollen, and he wasn't in any hurry to summon up any more control.

Dani, however, seemed to have held on to more brain function than he had.

Because the first thing out of those kissable lips was, "Why were you blushing, baby?"

Maybe it was the baby.

Perhaps it was that he'd suddenly become a living, breathing bag of blood existing only for this woman.

Or possibly his filter had been erased at the same time that the spice of cinnamon had hit his tongue.

But whatever the reason, Ethan found himself telling her the truth.

"I have a library fantasy."

Her chin jerked, eyes going wide. "Care to elaborate?"

His brain started working, right about the time she rose on tiptoe and her mouth came to his, searing him with a blazing kiss that made his legs tremble as though Fanny had just put his ass through the worst sort of drills on the ice.

"Ethan?" she asked when she dropped back down.

"Yeah?"

"What's the fantasy?"

And hell, if it got her close to him, had her body flush to his, her mouth on his then he'd tell her every last fantasy he'd harbored over the months and years.

"You in a short skirt and knee-highs, bending over the reference stack while I fuck you from behind."

She froze.

Fuck.

Too strong. Too fast. Too much.

He'd just gotten her used to him sitting next to her on the bus and plane, had finally secured a date. He wasn't supposed to skip over the rest of the first-date-getting-to-know-you stuff and dive straight into role play and fantasies.

"I—"

Her thumb brushed over his bottom lip. "Would I wear my glasses?"

His cock twitched, a groan tumbling out of his mouth.

She smiled, no sign of shy. Only a confident, smart, sexy as fuck woman standing plastered against him. "I'm reading that as a yes."

He bent his head, desperate for just one more brief taste of that spicy and sweet.

"Yes," he said, when he managed to pull back. "You'd wear the fucking glasses, sweetheart."

Her eyes were glazed, but her smile was fucking gorgeous. "Okay, then."

"Okay," he murmured, his hand shifting to cup the side of her neck, the other clenched on the sumptuous curve of her hip. He stared into her eyes, at her face, tracing every millimeter, committing the faint scar crisscrossing her left brow to memory, making a mental note to ask her at some later point where she'd gotten it. Ethan wanted to know everything about her. Her eyelashes were so long, nearly touching the skin of her cheekbones, her top lip plump, fading from almost maroon to a lighter mauve as it dipped inward. Her earlobes were attached and pierced, though he'd never seen her wear earrings and made another mental note to find out if, like her glasses, she just didn't wear them to work, or if she didn't wear them at all.

"Ethan?" she asked what could have easily been centuries later.

He couldn't be counted on to keep track of meaningless things like time when he held this woman.

"Yeah?"

"Weren't you going to take me somewhere?"

He blinked, mentally shook himself.

And then he found the control to release her, to lace their fingers together. "Yeah, I am."

———

"Is this a kidnapping?" Dani asked as he tucked her into the car he'd managed to borrow from a buddy. Ethan had planned ahead, had his friend leave the small SUV at the arena, and would be doing Tim "a favor" by returning it to the amphitheater so Tim would have it when he got off his shift that ended—

Ethan's eyes flicked to the dash.

Twenty minutes ago.

Meh, Tim was a good guy. They'd played in college together, and Tim had gone on to managing bands, and eventually when he'd had a family, managing venues, including this one outside of Denver.

So now, Ethan's friend had a municipal job (the city technically maintained the amphitheater) with good benefits and a pension, a wife and three kids, and a soft spot for a man (Ethan) trying to win the heart of an incredible woman. Oh, along with the clearance to let visitors into the park after hours for a romantic date.

Keys. Romance. Check. Check.

And in return, Ethan had scored Tim and his family tickets to the Red Wings versus Avs game. Good seats, too. Club level, just two rows behind the glass.

He could have gotten better for a Gold game, but—gasp— Tim's favorite team was not the one that Ethan was currently playing on.

So much for friendship, huh?

Fingers on his cheek startled him, and he realized he'd been quiet as he navigated his way to the freeway. Starting the date off right by ignoring the woman he was supposed to be wooing. Way to go.

"I like when you smile," Dani whispered. "It's like a surprise hidden in your beard, only revealed if someone looks close enough."

He captured her wrist, pressed a kiss to her palm. "The first time you smiled at *me,* I almost ran into a pole."

"What?"

"I'd been trying to get you to notice me for months, to really look at me." He laughed. "But it seemed like you were completely indifferent, even though I was burning up for you. You're quiet, but I always felt like there was so much more going on in your head than the rest of the world could see—"

A snort. "Yeah. Like crippling social anxiety."

"I like you, just the way you are." Another kiss to her palm before he placed her hand down on his thigh. "Anyway, back to my pining. Max was teasing you like he teases everyone, and then suddenly you came back with some quip about his game and how your character 'had significantly more melee than his pathetic excuse for a paladin,' and Max froze, his face warring between shock and horror. I laughed, because I'm a cruel asshole, and then you glanced up, gave me a full look at those gorgeous eyes for the first time, and I . . ."

"What?"

Fell for her. Right then and there.

Vowed that he'd win her over, would own her heart.

Because she owned his.

But that was too much too soon. So, he needed to temper it back, return to first date vibes.

"I knew that I had to get to know the woman who decimated Max's video game prowess."

She chuckled. "Do you want to know something?"

He wanted to know *everything*.

But first date, and all that. Yadda, yadda, yadda.

Which was why he just nodded instead.

"The truth is that I didn't even play that game. I was just really freaking tired of hearing him blabber on about it." A shrug. "Luckily, I knew enough about it that I was able to fool him."

Amusement was a coiled spring, one that unloaded, laughter bursting out of him as he took the exit that would take them off the highway and up toward the twisting road leading to the amphitheater. "You're devious."

"I couldn't believe he fell for it." Ethan saw one shoulder lift and fall out of the corner of his eye. "I actually felt guilty about it and wanted to tell him the truth."

Her palm on his leg squeezed. "Why didn't you?"

She was quiet for long enough that he expected her not to answer him. "Because of the way you looked at me."

He'd just turned into the driveway, saw Tim standing by the gate, and braked. "How did I look at you?"

"Like you saw me."

SEVENTEEN

DANI

"Like you see me."

The words had burst out of her in an unconscious blurt.

The truth.

But still, something that revealed too much.

Except . . . did it *truly* reveal too much? Ethan had been pretty fucking clear about how he felt about her, more now that she could recognize since she'd decided to yank the blinders off, grasp onto the attraction, the mutual like, and to take a leap of faith.

She'd spent so long being dissatisfied and lonely and sad.

Enough was finally enough.

She needed to buck up . . . or accept the loneliness.

And since that bitter isolation had grown to be a heavier burden, a tighter corset, squeezing the life from her more by the year, she'd bucked up.

Which meant she would have to accept that the whole bucking up process meant that she would be saying revealing things such as *like you see me.*

What she wasn't prepared for was his reaction to it.

The way the car slid to an abrupt stop, the emotion in his eyes when he snagged her hand from his thigh and brought it to his chest, resting it over the spot where his heart pounded below—a rapid *thrum-thrum* that matched her own pulse.

"I see you, sweetheart," he murmured. "And it's the prettiest fucking thing I've ever had the privilege to lay eyes on."

Thrum-thrum.

Thrum-thrum.

Thrum—

Knock-knock.

She jumped, the seat belt tightening around her shoulder, heart pounding for a completely different reason. Ethan's lips formed a curse, and then he gently released her hand and turned to lower the window.

"Hey, Tim," he said, shaking hands with the man who'd approached the car. "Thanks for doing this."

"You sure you don't want me to hang around and drive you back?"

Ethan shook his head. "I've got it covered."

"All right then." He released Ethan's hand, tapped on the frame of the door, eyes coming to Dani, and his lips turning up. Even in the dim illumination from the moonlight, she could see he was a handsome man with thick, dark hair and a winning smile along with curiosity written all over his face. Though to his credit, he didn't probe, just nodded at her in hello and said, "Park up ahead." Another tap. "Everything's ready for you."

Then he stepped back, and Ethan drove forward, parking in the shadows next to something that appeared dark and forbidding —except if she squinted and turned her head to the side, she could see a few lights up at the top.

"Why do I feel like I should circle back to questioning you about your kidnapping tactics?" she asked as Ethan came around and opened her door. "Is this where you take women who've pried out your deepest darkest fantasies as punishment?"

He ran a finger over her cheek. "That one fantasy is hardly the deepest and darkest one I have about you."

A little shiver of heat skated along her spine. "What other ones do you have?"

His hand found her waist, drew her close. "Why don't you tell me one of yours?" More heat, embers coalescing into tendrils, those threads growing and twining together into a thick, heavy rope.

Her cheeks were hot.

Her pussy was wet.

But that was beside the point.

Well, maybe, maybe not, because one point—a really important one—was that she wanted him. Badly. The other important point was that even with the desire burning within her, a perpetually burning flame that threatened to incinerate her, she wasn't sure if she could share any of her fantasies with this man.

They were too deeply entrenched, hidden behind walls she wasn't sure she could allow him to breach . . .

This was still too fresh and difficult to accept.

And . . . maybe she was just too shy.

The backs of his knuckles brushed her cheeks, drawing her focus to his face, to the clean lines cut by his beard, the silver cast of his skin from the moonlight, the flash of white teeth when he smiled gently at her. "Rain check?"

"Wh-what?" she sputtered.

"Rain check on whatever fantasy or fantasies are bouncing around that brain of yours."

His light tone had her smiling. "I'm neither agreeing nor disagreeing to this."

Another brush of those knuckles. "I think I can tempt it out of you."

"You could try."

Laughter, warm and heady, filled the night air as he tugged her up an incline. "I think I might know a way to succeed."

He was probably right. Hell, he *was* right. Ethan most definitely could find a way to tug the information out of her mind.

"Rain check," she murmured.

A husky chuckle. "Deal, sweetheart."

"Tell me about your parents?"

He nodded, shifting her closer, and Dani found herself resting her head on his chest. She was far too short for it to rest on his shoulder, but it felt nice to be nestled in the crook between arm and side, for the sound of his steady pulse to fill her eardrum, his voice rumbling through his body, vibrating against her as he answered her question.

"Mom's so fucking smart that sometimes I feel like I only understand half of what she's saying, especially when she's talking about something with regards to her work," he said, his voice filled with a warmth that she was coming to recognize.

Because she'd felt it directed at her.

"What does she do?"

"Russian literature and its intersection with early eighteenth-century American works."

Dani paused. "I only understood half of that."

He kissed the top of her head. "Join the club."

"And your dad?"

"He's also a professor. His specialty is higher mathematics. Think calculus but on steroids." A laugh. "I understand even less of his work. It has more letters and symbols than numbers."

"Sounds intense."

"It is." He smoothed back her hair. "And they ended up with a son who is an athlete. Two of the great brains of their time, and you've got me."

There was an interesting note in his tone, but it wasn't remarkable in a good way. Instead, it bristled along her skin, making her feel as though she'd been yanked backward through a hedge. It spoke to the insecurity inside her, called like to like, and . . . she fucking hated it.

She spun into him, halting him in his tracks, bringing their bodies flush against one another. They'd reached the top of the slope, and her eyes needed a moment to adjust, to see what was in his eyes.

More bristling.

"What's that?" she asked, waving a hand at his face.

"What's what?" he countered.

"That tone. That expression." She cupped his cheeks, made easier since she was at the top of the incline and he was a foot behind her, the angle aligning their faces. "Do you think for one second that your parents aren't proud of you? That you haven't done something fucking incredible?"

He turned his head, kissed her palm. "I just shoot a puck at a net and get in an occasional fight on the ice. It's nothing as important as the work they're doing," he said. "Nor even as important as yours. I'm a cog that can be replaced. An athlete with a shelf life, and that's just fact. They're discovering knowledge, helping others gain it. You're aiding in the running of this big machine, helping dozens, if not more people be successful and have jobs and make a living." He peeled her hands off, wove their fingers together. "Without me, they'd be fine. Without *you*, without others, they'd be lost."

There was a lot to unpack there.

Starting with the fact that she'd never quite been able to articulate anything close to what he'd just said, even though she had felt the same way too many fucking times over the course of her life.

But it was funny.

She'd found herself growing a lot over the last days, identifying the painful memories, understanding their hold on her, finding the courage to begin taking baby steps forward. And now hearing that same note of pain in Ethan's voice was like leaping backward, falling into a dark hole, hating that someone could feel that way about themselves.

And if she hated that *he* could feel that way, how had she lived for so freaking long feeling the same?

It was . . . enlightening.

Frustrating.

Infuriating.

Illuminating.

"You are a wonderful, smart, talented, lovely man. You are more than a cog in a machine. You're . . . Ethan, and I feel so lucky to know you."

His lips parted, a shuddering breath slipping out and coating her skin. "Dani," he murmured, his tone almost pained.

"You see," she whispered. "I was accosted outside my office by a man, who dropped my treasured tablets on the ground, and then again by him outside the library where he stole my books. And again in a hall where he stole my bags of rocks"—his mouth curved—"and that man, well . . . he's pretty fucking amazing. He gave me the courage to peek at the memories I'd locked down, to release them and their hold on me. It was terrifying, letting go of that safety net." She squeezed his hands. "But I found it wasn't so scary when I understood that he'd be patiently waiting to catch me."

Another of those breaths, stuttering and staccato, a big chest practically vibrating against her.

Then his hands wove into her hair, and he kissed her.

The man had a fucking glorious mouth, soft and plump, ringed by the short bristles of his beard. Rough and smooth, no caution in the way he held her, how he plundered her lips.

But eventually, they had to breathe, so she pulled back, reveling in the way he held her face in his calloused hands. "I told you that you could do anything that you put your mind to."

"I'm starting to believe that."

His forehead rested against hers for a heartbeat.

Then he took her hands again and tugged her forward. "Come on then. Our first date awaits."

He spun her around, tugged her around the edge of the building . . .

And quite simply, she fell in love.

A small, round table sat near an opening in a plain white railing, the gap showing a staircase leading down to a gorgeous stone amphitheater. "It's Red Rocks," she whispered, as he led her to the table. "I've always wanted to come here for a concert."

He tugged out her chair. "We'll have to come back for one."

When he pushed it in, lights turned on, shining up along the burnished rust-colored stone walls, soft music filling the space. It swept up those stairs like a thunderstorm, a low rumble that bounced along the rock, quivered through her abdomen, filling her with the gentle melody of one of her favorite pop songs.

"How did you know?" she whispered.

"I've seen you perk up when it comes on during warm-up."

"How?" she asked again.

She shouldn't even have been there, had been sneaking out because she was desperate to catch a glimpse of him while he'd skated. Instead, she should have been prepping for the game, not mooning over him.

He sat down across from her, took her hand. "How could I not?" A squeeze. "How could I not notice you?"

Dani melted into a puddle of goo.

Either that or she fell a little bit more in love with him.

Then he lifted the silver cover on the plate between them, and there was no doubt, she'd plummeted into love with this man.

Eighteen

Ethan

The Lyft deposited them outside the hotel lobby, and he felt a kind of peace he'd not experienced before as they walked inside and headed for the elevators.

He would have liked it better had they been going up to a room they shared, but for now, he rode the elevator to her floor, walked her to her door, and stole several more kisses.

She threaded her fingers into his belt loops, tugged him close. "Come inside."

Ah, a statement that could be taken so many ways.

Alas, they were still riding First Date vibes, so he said goodnight.

Then went down to his room, jerked off, and fell headlong into sleep.

———

The knock on his door in the morning was unwelcome, but he stumbled to the peephole, stared through it . . . and suddenly, it was a lot more welcome.

He pulled open the wooden panel. "Hey, sweetheart," he said, knowing his voice was raspy.

Her eyes went wide, and Ethan watched her throat work as she swallowed. "I—"

"You okay?"

Her gaze slid down, a heated, tangible thing that had him remembering he was only wearing boxer briefs. When her stare stayed down, he allowed his own gaze to drop, saw that he was sporting some intense morning wood, even more than normal considering the need for this woman that was a fire coursing through his veins.

"I—I'm—"

Warm hands on his chest.

Warm hands shoving him—not gently. He was so surprised, he stumbled back several paces, and then the door was slamming closed, and Dani was launching herself into his arms.

And her mouth was on his.

Flames bursting to life, coating his skin, burning him to ash.

A warm, curvy woman against him, her hands stroking every inch of him as she continued shoving him, forcing him to retreat . . . until the backs of his legs hit the bed.

He tumbled onto the mattress, his hands coming around her hips, drawing her over him, her thighs straddling his. "Ethan?" she murmured.

Her hands were on his skin, on his *naked* skin. Her pussy hot and damp even through his underwear and the black leggings she wore.

"Yeah?" he replied gruffly.

"Are you okay?" she whispered.

"No," he admitted. "I'm not okay."

She drifted closer. "What's the matter?"

"I'm trying to remember that we've only gone on one date," he said.

"And?" she asked, when he didn't say anything else.

"And I'm trying to remember that, so I don't strip you naked, flip us over, and get my mouth between those fucking gorgeous thighs of yours."

Her breath shuddered out. Then she inhaled sharply. "Ethan?" she asked again on the next exhale.

"Yeah?" he said again.

"Do you really want to do that?"

He moved, an abrupt action that he seemingly had no control over, snagging her hand, tugging it down until it rested against the hard jut of his erection currently tenting the front of his underwear. "I'm fucking desperate to do that," he said, groaning when her fingers convulsed. "But I also know that we're just starting to get to know each other and—"

His words faltered.

Because she reared back and yanked her shirt over her head. Then reached behind her, unhooked her bra . . .

And let it fall to the floor.

"Yes, please," she said.

"Y-yes"—he choked—"please?"

"Yes, I want you to take me, to strip me." A beat, her lips turning up. "Well, the *rest* of me, and—"

Words failed him, but luckily action didn't. He flipped them, slanted his mouth across hers, cutting her off, knowing that if she uttered another sexy request, he was very likely to come in his boxer briefs. Aware that if she kept talking, he was going to lose control and forget he didn't have a fucking condom. Because she was *topless* and her breast were . . . fucking incredible, so much more glorious than he'd imagined—and he'd imagined a whole hell of a lot.

It would be so easy for him to lose his underwear, to yank off her leggings, and then he could be plunging home and—

Her lips found his, and they rolled on the mattress, his body pressing into hers, hers pressing into his, until eventually he managed to flip her again, to sink his body over hers, and even with their bottoms between them, it was the best fucking sensation of his life.

He trailed his hand along her side, and she threw her head back, the lines of her throat taut, the tendons in sharp relief, the slope calling to his mouth, and he heeded that call, dragging his lips along her skin, inhaling the scent of strawberries, tasting that sweetness on his tongue.

She moaned, gripped his shoulders, her nails digging in slightly when he reached the part where her neck met the slender curve of her collarbone.

Pausing, he spoke against the delicate divot. "You like that?"

Her eyes slid down, met his, and he expected her to shy away, to pull back, to do . . . something that wasn't wrapping her legs around his waist, her hips undulating against him, her words and gaze steady when she murmured, "Yes, Ethan. I like that." Her hand drifted up, cupped his jaw. "I—I—" She faltered for just a moment, and then he watched determination firm the gentle lines of her face. "I like *you*."

His cock was hard, aching, but what he felt for this woman was more than just desire and need.

Or perhaps, it was need in a different way.

To just be with her. To understand all the little idiosyncrasies that made Dani *Dani*.

So much tenderness and curiosity and affection, and while he knew her in many ways already—he knew she was a woman a man kept, knew she was someone who he'd cut out his heart for—he also wanted to know all the little things about her. What made her laugh, what made her sad. The places she wanted to travel. The books that made her cry and long for more. He wanted to glean every tiny detail because she was utterly fascinating. And as much as he couldn't wait until he knew all those parts of her, he was also looking forward to the journey, to the slow, incremental learning.

Which probably couldn't happen if she was topless in his hotel bed, but . . .

She was topless. Beneath him. With only leggings and some underwear between them.

And she wanted his mouth on her.

So he'd know her that way before the rest of it.

"I like you, too," he murmured. "Probably more than I should." Given how short a time she'd been allowing him in to see the real Dani.

Her lips tipped up. "I don't think you're supposed to admit that to the woman you're on top of."

He bent, nipped at her bottom lip. "It's better than liking you less than I should."

Amusement had been glittering in her eyes, that mouth curved, but his words made her pause, just for a brief moment, the delight flattening out, turning the warmth in those irises cool, unfeeling.

Then she smiled again, wider this time, but it was missing all the warmth, all the delight from before.

"What is it?" he asked, knowing this was one of those things that time hadn't yet granted him the opportunity to learn.

She wrapped her arms around his shoulders, fingers gripping his hair. "Kiss me."

An order.

One he obliged, slanting his mouth across hers, absorbing the wonder of this woman and how she tasted, how she felt, how she made everything inside him realign in a completely different way. But even as he kissed her, he shifted them to the side, tugging her so she was cradled against his chest when they broke apart for air. He couldn't stop himself from running his hand up and down her spine, bit back a groan when she slipped her palm between them, trailing warm fingers along his abdomen.

"Why'd you stop?" she murmured.

"What did I say?" he asked. "That hurt you?"

"Nothing." She smiled again, pressed her mouth to his, kissing him deeply, until his lungs were straining for air, until his cock was aching, his fingers trembling, desire hazing his vision, turning the edges red. Until he was wondering why in the fuck he was pushing this, why he wasn't just getting back to the tumbling and kissing and licking every single inch of her part.

But . . . he needed to know why she'd gotten sad.

Because he didn't want to be the one who hurt her. Not *ever*.

"Dani," he whispered, tearing his lips from hears.

She sighed, closed her eyes. "Please, Ethan."

That *please* almost broke him. It was just . . . he had to do the right thing here, had to be himself, and he wasn't the type of guy who pretended to not know the truth, who dismissed it just because he had a boner, and it would be easier *not* to talk about it.

Did he want her? Fuck yes.

Did he want her pain between them when he had her? No.

He didn't want that coloring their interactions, her pleasure, their time together in each other's arms.

She meant more than a quick fuck.

She meant *everything*.

It was as simple as that.

He squeezed her shoulder. "Tell me, sweetheart."

Her chin dropped to her chest. "Why can't you just take advantage of the half-naked woman in your arms?"

He stroked a hand over her hair, told her the truth. "Because I don't want to take advantage of you. Ever." Fingers under her chin, drawing it up so that her gaze was on his. "And I want to know you. Even the sad pieces. The hurt and broken. Give them to me. Let me help you put them back together."

Lips parting, a shaking sigh coating his skin. She shifted closer, her mouth a hairsbreadth from his. "You're not taking advantage of me."

He ran his thumb over her bottom lip. "I don't want to hurt you."

"You're not." But there it was again, the falter. The hint of pain.

"Yet," he said gently, cupping her cheek. "That's the part you're not saying, isn't it? I haven't hurt you *yet*."

She went still and then sighed again, caution edging into her expression. "Should I remind you that I'm still half-naked and waiting for you to do the whole kissing every inch of me part?"

"I want to," he said. *Fuck*, he wanted to.

"But . . ." she whispered after he didn't say anything else.

"But . . ."

He needed her to tell him every detail of her past? Fuck, that made him an even bigger asshole than spending the last minutes ignoring the lusciousness of her curves and the blatant invitation in her words, her eyes. She'd already shared so much, and besides that, she didn't owe him an explanation of her past, not even because she'd offered up her body, allowed him close, had gone on a date with him, had told him what had happened in high school.

The truth was that she didn't owe him anything. Period.

And frankly, he hadn't earned enough of her trust to expect anything.

He had to believe that they would get there, that he'd unlock her inner core with patience and perseverance. She'd already given him so much in the short time they'd been together. "But, nothing," he said gently. "I'll be here, ears available for when you're ready to tell me."

Still.

Dani could go so perfectly still. Like a beautiful statue rather than a living, breathing woman. Of course, she was a statue with a stare that bored into him. "You're beautiful," he whispered, brushing the backs of his knuckles over her throat.

She unfroze, her hands coming to his cheeks, a blip of pain trailing across her face. It was gone in an instant, and then her mouth was back on his.

"Charmer," she whispered.

"Truth," he whispered back.

NINETEEN

Truth.

He'd just whispered the word like it was the most obvious thing in the world.

Even though it wasn't true, couldn't be true.

Despite the progress she'd made, she knew she wasn't beautiful, and most of the time she certainly didn't feel beautiful on the inside or the out. She was just Dani, just a woman, who'd been so fucking lonely and scared and filled with shards of broken glass and twisted memories that she hadn't been living—

She was half-naked, and Ethan was holding her.

She'd gone on a date, had talked to him like a woman talked to a man, hadn't panicked—or not much anyway.

And perhaps it wouldn't seem like a lot to other people, perhaps it was the smallest baby step to the outside world. But to her . . .

She'd taken a giant leap forward.

So she was going to damned well go with that.

She brushed her tongue along the seam of his mouth, dipping

it inside when he parted his lips, tangling it with his. His groan sent tingles through her nerves, dipped down between her thighs.

He rolled them again, pressing her down into the mattress, his body heavy and hard. His hand slid down her side, cupping her hip, slipping beneath her leggings to take one globe of her ass in his rough palm. The hot brand had her gasping, her pelvis tilting, wanting him closer, even though he was wearing far too many clothes.

He was wearing one item of clothing.

It was still too many.

Speaking of which, she shoved down her leggings, their limbs tangling as she kicked them off her feet, as she shimmied her panties down behind them. And since his chest was right there, she took the opportunity to kiss it.

His skin tasted of sunshine and the gentle, cool breeze that gathered on one's skin just before the sun started to set.

Lower and lower.

Until his chest existed only for her gaze and mouth, until he halted her explorations before she could taste every inch of him like she desired. Capturing her hands in one of his, he brought them up to his mouth, kissed the back of them, dragged his teeth along the sensitive insides of her wrists.

She shivered, flexed against his grip. "I want to touch."

"And I don't want to come in my underwear," he countered, lips moving up her forearm, light kisses along the way until he made it to the inside of her elbow, and fuck her if that spot didn't seem to have a direct line connecting straight to her pussy.

A shudder wracked her frame before she could tease him about his threats of prematurity. "You could come *in* me," she said breathlessly, as he continued kissing up her arm and then down her chest, drifting closer and closer to the hard buds of her nipples.

He froze, groaned, dropping his forehead to her collarbone. "Killing me, sweetheart."

"I'm the naked one," she said.

"Exactly," he said. "And *I'm* the one without a condom. So, I'll say again"—his finger trailed down her chest—"killing. *Me.*"

"Is that all?"

He sputtered, and her amusement was a joyful, buoyant thing, setting her heart fluttering, her lips twitching. "Is—"

She nudged him back, sliding from the bed.

Somehow, she didn't feel self-conscious striding over to her purse, where it had fallen when she'd gone all cavewoman by the door, unzipping it and pulling out her emergency toiletry kit. Probably because when she glanced over her shoulder, it was to see his hot gaze on her, desire evident on his face. No derision. No disgust.

Just wanton need.

And she suddenly wasn't shy.

It was like all the heavy, gaudy varnish on a piece of furniture was sanded off, the beautiful grain of the wood below finally visible.

She was . . . finally *herself.*

"You're doing makeup at a time like this?" Ethan asked, his tone light, making her realize that she'd been acting like a statue again, bag open in one hand, a tube of lipstick in the other.

She tossed the latter aside, clenched the bag in her hand. "It's your fault," she muttered, climbing onto the bed next to him.

He was lying there like a tasty morsel she wanted to taste every inch of.

"*What's* my fault?"

"You're too fucking attractive." More muttering, though this time it was accompanied by her rustling through the contents of her bag. "Too damned distracting."

"I'll circle back to your need for my sexy body in a moment." He sat up, trailed his fingers along her shoulder. "For now, tell me what you're looking for."

"I'm . . . looking . . . for . . . ah-ha!" Her fingers closed around the plastic square, she pulled it out with a flourish and held out the condom. "This!"

His lips turned up. His eyes went even hotter. "You're a fucking goddess."

More joy bubbling inside her. So much that her face actually hurt from smiling so wide. "This, I know," she said lightly, thinking that in this moment, in this bed, with this man, she really *could* be a goddess, could go after what she wanted and not be a fucking coward. "I'm—"

His mouth found hers for a kiss that stole her breath, had her melting down to the mattress, him coming on top of her.

"You taste like temptation," he murmured, kissing his way back down her chest. "And the woman who has captured my soul." Those words bounced around her chest, bringing pleasure in their wake. Love and need and desire all wound together, lifting her higher than she ever thought possible. His lips dragging over her skin as she basked in that, his heated, damp mouth a fraction of an inch from her nipple.

"I—" His head lowered. "Oh, God—"

She groaned, lost her train of thought for long minutes as he lavished her breasts with attention, before slowly drifting lower. Her hands found his hair, stalling his downward progress when she found a particularly sensitive spot.

He obliged her unspoken request, stroking and kissing, nipping and tracing the area beneath her ribs, delving into her belly button, using his tongue and lips to create patterns on her skin that had her nerves prickling, her temperature rising. Fingers and mouth along the curve of her stomach, over her hip bones, drifting down between her thighs, coaxing them apart and settling his shoulders between them.

And then he paused, hot breath on her pussy, hands beneath her ass. "Yes?" he asked, his voice a rasp that made her nipples bead tightly, her toes curl against the mattress.

"Yes," she breathed.

"Thank fuck," he said, the curse against her labia, vibrating through her, gathering slick heat in her center, taking her dangerously close to an orgasm even before his tongue traced through her folds.

That single slide through her pussy was the best sensation of her life.

One that was quickly eclipsed by the next, and then the next, and then the *next*, desire pooling, need spiraling higher as he ground his mouth against her and set about wringing every drop of pleasure from her body. Her head fell back, her hips bucked against his lips, moans tumbling from her mouth one after another.

That beard . . .

Fuck, it was *everything*.

Sensitizing her nerve endings, ramping her pleasure. She gripped his head, held him tight, and just hung on for the ride.

And what an incredible ride it was. She was shooting through the sky like a rocket taking off. Not a gentle slope to that precipice. It was straight the fuck up, and her engines were firing on all fucking cylinders until . . .

Boom.

Explosion.

It began at her clit, his mouth latched tight, his tongue flicking rapidly against the bundle of nerves. Then that wave of pleasure spread like a tsunami, flowing through her folds, clenching tight against the finger he'd pushed deep, was curling up against her g-spot. Every muscle in her body went taut for one brief moment and then lax as bliss flowed through her.

"Fuck," she whispered, going limp against the mattress. "Fucking *hell*."

Ethan prowled up her body, gathered her into his arms, one palm smoothing her hair back. "Fuck, is right," he murmured, his mouth moving to her ear, nipping lightly at the lobe, his words making her shiver. "Fucking hell, you're the sexiest woman I've ever been given the privilege to lay eyes on."

Gravel in his voice, whispering over her skin, fanning the fires between her thighs. She rolled them, pushing him back to the bed, leaning down and slanting her mouth across his.

The sleek dart of his tongue, the soft sting of his teeth against her bottom lip, his kiss was sustenance and torture. Her lungs screamed for oxygen, but she could get enough air by kissing her way across his chest, sucking it in through her nose as she laved the divot of his throat, used her teeth lightly at his nipples. His muscles grew harder with each inch of skin she paid homage to, until he felt as hard as granite beneath her.

She kissed her way down, lower and lower until . . .

"There you are, gorgeous," she murmured.

His cock was pressed against the front of his boxer briefs, its glistening head just barely poking out the top, and she gave in to the urge to taste that moisture, flicking her tongue out to lap up the salty drop.

The brackish flavor had barely hit her taste buds before she found herself on her back, Ethan on top of her. His color was high, his hair tumbled, his beard slightly askew, but it was the way he was looking at her that had her thighs clenching around his.

Slowly, his hand slid up her side, the rough callouses on his palm making her squirm, especially when he trailed it in, pausing right below her breast.

"Eth," she murmured, trying to shift so that it would move just a few inches higher.

He smiled, but there wasn't anything amused about it.

She felt like the seal swimming frantically for shore, a Great White circling beneath, readying to strike.

If his cock brought her as much pleasure as his mouth had earlier, she was in very good hands . . . penises? Teeth? Tongue? Hands again? All of the above. *Ha.*

That desire tempered, his smile softening. "What?" he murmured, tracing the edge of her mouth with his thumb. She realized her amusement must have bled over into a smirk.

"I was thinking I was in good hands"—her gaze dropped—"or cocks."

That cock in question twitched against her. "As in plural?"

She swatted at him. "You know what I mean." Then arched a brow. "Unless you keeping your underwear on means you have something you need to tell me?"

He shoved his boxers down, his cock springing forth. "Nothing to fear on that front."

She clamped a hand to her chest, feigned swooning. "Well, thank God for that."

"Thank *God* for your tits and the way they jiggle when you do that."

"Thank God," she countered, loving his expression—the open need, the desperate desire sharpening the edges of his face—as she reached for his cock, stroking a finger over the velvety head. "For your single penis. Because I need it inside me."

He cursed, using far more creative language than she'd anticipated.

"Wow," she breathed.

His lips found a spot behind her ear, one so sensitive that she felt her pussy clench. "Wow, what?"

She turned her head, halted with her mouth a hairsbreadth from his. "I like it when you talk dirty to me." A hand sliding down his stomach. "Remember how you asked me if I always stroke things so carefully?" Her fingers wrapped around him, squeezed. "I promise, I do."

Another curse, Ethan letting his weight come down on top of her, trapping her hand between them. Not that she minded, especially considering she had it wrapped around his cock.

"I don't think you're shy at all," he murmured, lips finding her throat and sucking deeply.

"I don't feel sh-shy," she said, the fingers of her other hand drifting up his spine, slipping into the short locks, gripping tight. "With you, I feel like I can just be Dani."

Motionless.

He took a turn to play statue and froze on top of her.

For just a single heartbeat. Then his mouth was on hers, and she was being devoured again, that strong, powerful shark threatening to swallow her whole. His hands were on her ass, her hips, her breasts, cupping her cheek so he could kiss her deeper and harder and—

He pulled back, one hand flat on the bed next to her face, the other on her jaw. "That is the sexiest thing you could have ever said to me."

"Eth—"

Another kiss that stole her breath, only this time she was ready for the intense, demanding man on top of her. She kissed him back, glad when he lifted up enough so she could use her formerly trapped hand to fondle his cock. He groaned into her mouth, hips jerking forward.

"I should probably warn you that it's been a while," he said, another groan tumbling from his lips as she showed him how well she could stroke.

"Then get inside me and make it less of *a while*."

He swallowed. "Dani," he growled. "I'm trying to make this good for you."

"I don't need good"—not strictly true, but she needed this man inside her, and if his oral skills were any indication, she already *knew* it would be fan-fucking-tastic, so he didn't have anything to worry about—"I just need *you*."

"We don't have to rush," he said, and every syllable was strained.

But seriously, the man didn't look like he could spend all day like this, teasing and coaxing their pleasure higher and higher. He looked ready to explode. And she wanted that explosion inside her.

"Inside me," she whispered, aloud this time.

"Fuck, sweetheart," he gritted. Sweat gleamed on his forehead, his chin dropped to his chest, lungs sawing in and out. His palm fell from her cheek, dropping to the bed beside her head, the tendons and muscles on his forearms taut and pressing against skin.

Fuck, what was it about men's forearms that were so fucking sexy?

She rotated her head to the side, keeping her hand on the hard length of his erection, pumping up and down, but giving in to the urge that had filled her at the sight of his strength by sinking her teeth into the muscles, not firmly enough to hurt, but enough that she could taste the salt and spice of his skin, feel the power of those arms in her mouth.

He jerked, more curses tumbling from his mouth.

And a second later, her hand was tugged from his cock, and he was grabbing the condom she'd retrieved.

She wanted to roll it down the length of him, but he was too quick, tearing into the corner of the plastic square with his teeth, yanking the condom out, and covering his cock with it in the next moment.

Then he knelt between her thighs and paused with his erection . . . so . . . fucking . . . close.

"Are you su—"

She gripped his ass, tugging down while at the same time jerking up, and that first stretch of him filling her was the best pleasure-pain of her existence. It had been a long time for her, too, and no one had ever felt like Ethan. Wide and beyond hard, pressing deep, spreading her thighs wide as he stroked his way all . . . the . . . way . . . home.

"Fuck," she said on an exhale.

That was . . .

"Incredible," he murmured, dropping to his elbows, his mouth finding hers for a scorching kiss as he pumped deep and slow and steady. "You're so fucking beautiful," he said when their lips fell apart, when she arched back, her neck straining, pleasure coiling, her hips rising to meet his in a rhythm that was set to send her straight into her first-ever double orgasm.

"*Ethan*," she whispered when he hit something, some place really, *really* good. "Baby, I—"

His eyes locked onto hers, staring deeply, seeming to read into the urgency in her tone because he kept moving in that inexorable way, with firm, sure strokes, only they grew faster and harder, and she felt sweat bead on her skin, her lips tingle, her muscles grow tight as the ache inside her grew and expanded. Her breathing sped, that edge was right there, and then . . . he slipped a hand between them, lightly caressed that bundle of nerves at the apex of her thighs.

And . . .

She exploded.

Fuck, that was good.

But good grew as Ethan sped up, hips pistoning, thrusting deeper, a growl bubbling up in his throat, every time he bottomed out, her orgasm flared anew, fresh sparks of pleasure scattering through her, shooting stars of sensation until he groaned her name, thrust once, twice more, and—

Collapsed on top of her.

He was heavy, making it hard for her to breathe, but she didn't mind, actually liked the feel of him surrounding her, pressing her into the mattress. She loved the fact that he'd lost it so much that he was unaware, especially when he'd been careful the whole time with his strength. There was something so incredibly sexy in him not being in control.

"Sorry," he murmured, wrapping his arms around her and rolling them so she was sprawled across his chest.

She was feeling too relaxed to summon any words. Instead, she just nuzzled into his embrace, smiling when he tugged the blanket up and over them.

"You okay?" he murmured sometime later.

Her eyes were sliding closed, sleep threatening to take her under, and she must have managed some sort of reply because he chuckled as the blankets crept higher. Distantly, she was aware of the bed shifting, of Ethan walking to the bathroom to deal with the condom.

Then he was back, tugging her into his arms.

She stirred, feeling like she should summon the energy to say *something*.

"Sleep," he ordered, smoothing his hand up and down her spine.

"We should get up," she murmured.

"Sleep," he ordered again. "Just for a little while." His hand continued moving, and with that slow and steady rhythm, with his warm, hard body surrounding hers, that was an order she didn't mind obeying in the least.

Her eyes slid closed.

TWENTY

ETHAN

It was ten days later, they were in Baltimore for their twice-yearly matchup, and he was kissing Dani in the hall.

Where anyone might see.

But it was before the game, and she'd just agreed to go to a late dinner with his parents after the game.

From first date to casually dating to meeting his parents.

All in the span of less than two weeks.

So yeah, Ethan was feeling high on life.

Of course, it had taken him years to work up the courage to make that first move, years he was kicking himself doubly for, considering how good these couple of weeks had been.

From the library to this hall.

He loved spending time with Dani.

He just . . . plain loved Dani.

That wasn't a surprise. He'd been half in love with her from the moment he'd made her laugh at Max's expense all those months before. Now, he was firmly entranced, falling in deeper and deeper with every minute that passed, whether in her presence or not.

He loved making her laugh and smile. He fucking loved . . . fucking her. He'd gone out and invested in a giant box of condoms, and they managed to find themselves in one another's room most nights.

The sex was great.

But the rest of it was fantastic. How she forgot to be shy with him. How he could coax her to step out of her comfort zone if he kissed her just right. How she found the strength in herself to do the stepping without him. They filled their hours together with meals and movies, with learning all the little things.

So, fantastic was the minimum description he could muster.

And now, she was going to meet his parents.

It was going to be great. His mom would love her. His dad would clap him on the shoulder and beam and then later would whisper in his ear, asking him where in the fuck he'd found her because she was way too good for the likes of him.

Which was nothing more than the truth.

Dani was leaps and bounds above his level, so much more than he was worth and more than he deserved—

She pushed against his chest, lips swollen, chest heaving. "We need to get ready for the game."

That was true, but for the first time ever, he didn't want to play hockey. He wanted to skip on the game, to take this woman into a closet and make love with her, and then he wanted to introduce her to his parents.

Probably, he should reverse the order of things.

But the body wanted what the body wanted.

Which was why he tugged her close again.

"Ethan," she laughed.

"One more," he murmured. "Just one more."

"Oka—"

He cut her off with a kiss, held her tight until she pushed him away.

"Give a woman a chance to breathe."

"No, love," he said. "If you can breathe, then you can think, and pretty soon you'll start questioning why you're with a man like me."

Her face clouded. "Baby."

He hadn't meant it the way it sounded, and God knew he didn't suffer from a confidence problem. But once the sentiment was in the air, he couldn't deny that it was the truth—at least a little bit. Hell, even in his mental conversation with his parents, the same notion came up.

She was wonderful.

And he was damned lucky to have her.

"I'm being self-deprecating," he said. "That's all."

Her face gentled. "Well, don't tease like that. If I've made a promise to stop putting myself down, then you have to as well."

He ran his thumb back and forth along the inside of her wrist. "I can do that."

"Good." She swatted him on the ass. "Now go. Skate your butt off."

"Then you couldn't do *that*."

She grinned, knowing him losing his hockey butt was never at risk. It was a glorious side effect of the sport.

He released her, turned down the hall.

"Ethan?"

He spun back.

"Remember that I'm always watching."

Laughter bubbled in his chest.

She nibbled the corner of her mouth. "I didn't mean it like that."

Ethan had to steal one more kiss, to taste the chagrin on her lips. "I know," he murmured, nipping at her jaw. "I promise, I won't wink tonight."

He'd received no little amount of shit for his previous wink. Which meant that Dani had also received no little amount of shit for the same.

Same went for the ones he'd given her during every game since.

She groaned. "I hope that's true."

He bopped her on the nose. "It's not."

Another groan.

"See you after the game, love."

"Oh, God," she moaned. "I'm meeting your parents."

He kissed the fear off her lips. "They're going to love you," he promised.

"Go," she said, shoving him back. "Before I freak out even more."

"Leaving." A tug of her hair. "I'll try to get on some of those highlight reels." He patted her hip, turned away.

Quiet greeted him, all the way down the hall. Broken only when he nearly turned the corner.

Then she called, "See that you do."

He grinned, love for this woman filling him to the brim.

And Ethan found that when he hit the ice, he was still smiling.

———

Dani was a quiet statue at his back.

His mom and dad had taken turns hugging him and were now chattering his ear off.

"Honey, you played great," his mom said, "and then you did that . . . thing with the puck to get it up to . . . your teammate."

He laughed, squeezed her hand. She could wax poetic on Russian literature, but she couldn't distinguish a forehand pass from a backhand, let alone discerning between players as they moved rapidly on the ice. "Thanks, Mom," he said.

It had been a great game. The system working, riding the high of a series of goals from up and down the lineup. He felt like he was actually contributing and not just in working away from the puck. Ethan was connecting passes, making good defensive plays —he'd had a fire under his ass, both because Dani was watching and because his parents were there.

Things had just clicked, so Ethan was riding a definite high when he'd met up with Dani outside her office and had taken her to meet his parents.

A high that was so intoxicating it was certainly the reason for him missing what he really should have seen. Something he didn't recognize until later. Until it was too late to fix.

Until everything had changed.

"And who's this?" his dad asked.

Ethan turned and slipped an arm around Dani's waist, tugging her forward. "This is Dani."

His mom grinned, her brown curls a cloud around her head. "Hi, Dani, I'm Constance, and this is my husband, Brian." She stuck out a hand for Dani to shake. "It's so lovely to meet you. I feel like Ethan has been telling me about you for years."

Dani's lips parted, wide eyes coming to his.

He brushed his thumb over her cheek. "Someone might say that I've been a bit obsessed with you."

"For years?" she breathed.

A nod.

"Wow." She shifted closer, murmured, "Me, too."

And they'd wasted how much time circling each other? God, he should have made his move much sooner.

But his regret was something that would have to wait.

"I-it's nice to meet you," Dani stammered, and he watched her shake his mom's then his dad's hand. It was strange to hear the quiet voice, the shy taking over. She'd been so relaxed with him, so much *Dani* that he'd almost forgotten about the shy side of her.

He squeezed her waist. "Should we go to dinner?"

His dad nodded, eyes going from Dani to Ethan. "Yes, let's head out. We have reservations." He swept forward, wove his arm through Dani's, tugged her away from Ethan. "Is my son treating you well?"

"I—um—"

"Yes," his mom said, closing ranks on her other side. "Give me all the gory details. Has he brought you flowers? What about chocolates? Jewelry?"

"Those are all too cliché."

A scoff. "They may be cliché, but they're still beacons of romance."

"Cliché romance," he said, coming up behind them.

"Tell me, honey," his father murmured, "do I need to have a talk with my son about the merits of flowers and chocolates?"

Dani tossed a glance over her shoulder, fear in her expression.

He stepped forward, ready to move between them, to be a barrier between his parents and her discomfort, to shield her until she was prepared to speak.

But then her face changed, determination pushing out the fear.

"No," she murmured. "You don't have to have a talk with him."

"You sure?" his mom asked.

"I'm sure." Another glance, this one filled with warmth. "He bought me my favorite body wash." She leaned closer. "And then he planned a candlelight dinner for me at Red Rocks."

The first had drawn his mom's gaze to his, her brows arched fiercely. The second had made her face soften.

"That's my boy," she mouthed as his dad took over the conversation, saying something that had Dani laughing out loud, the lovely, ringing sound filling the hall.

And his heart.

And Ethan knew this was going to be the best night ever.

Twenty-One

Dani

She'd thought she was doing well, thought she'd managed to get past her insecurities because she was meeting people who loved Ethan.

And because *she* loved Ethan.

Dinner had gone well.

She'd started off a little slow, a bit stuttering, but once she really started listening, Constance had reminded her of her own mom. A force to be reckoned with, whip smart and funny, with plenty of pushy thrown in.

Then they'd dropped her and Ethan off at the hotel.

Or the initial plan was dropping them off, because they'd ended up staying for a drink in the bar, and that one drink had turned into three.

Dani had peeled off to use the bathroom, a little buzzed, more than a little high on life. She'd done her business in the single stall, had washed her hands, reached for the doorknob.

And then she'd heard it.

Well, *them*.

Voices in the hall, undoing everything she'd spent the last few weeks building up.

She recognized Brian's voice even through the door. "You've got a good one there, Eth."

Footsteps coming closer, their words rising in volume.

"I know I do."

The doorknob jiggled, making Dani jump, her hand clamping to her chest. The footsteps moved on, voices dimming, but not enough for her to miss hearing, "I love her, Dad. So fucking much."

"Oh shit," she whispered.

Shit. Shit. *Shit.*

Her knees gave way, and she sank to the floor, her ass hitting the cold tile. She should be happy. Thrilled even. She was helplessly in love with Ethan, had been for a while, even if she was good at pretending she wasn't.

Except . . . he *loved* her.

Fuck.

Her throat seized, spots flashing behind her lids, and her lungs worked without actually drawing oxygen into her bloodstream.

He loved her.

Fucking hell.

That . . . that . . . Her fingers scrambled for the lock, flicking it open, yanking the door wide. She stumbled out . . . right into Ethan.

Oh, fuck.

She wasn't ready for this.

She couldn't do this right now. She needed to have a panic attack in peace, needed to get to her room, to shove down all the old emotions of unworthiness that had burst forth at his words. It was just . . . too much and—

A soft hand on her back, rubbing up and down. "In and out," Ethan murmured. "In and out. That's it. You've got this."

Eventually, the edges of black receded, and she came back into herself in the hall, Ethan having tucked her close, his body wrapped tightly around hers. "You can't love me," she whispered. "You can't, you just can't."

His face gentled. "Except I do. I love you, Dani. Of course, I'd expected to tell you in a romantic setting, without the side of toilet. But I do." He cupped her cheek. "I love you."

She shook her head.

"Yes, baby. I do."

Her pulse thundered in her veins, her heart twisting this way and that. She needed a moment. She needed to think, to freak out, and then to recenter. To tell this man she loved him too.

"I love you, Dani," he murmured.

She pushed against his chest until he released her, staggering to her feet, shoving the hair out of her face. "I need—" She sucked in a breath. "I just need some time to—"

He rose with her, hands coming to her shoulders, eyes bright. "You don't need time. You need to accept that I love you." He jostled her lightly, making her head shake. "You have to—"

Her lungs went tight again.

The black crept back in.

"Just a second," she breathed, slipping out of his hold. "Ethan, this is so much. Too much. I need to think. I need to—"

Come to terms with the fact that her entire life had shifted on its axis again.

She loved the man, loved him back so intensely, but she couldn't muster the words out of her mouth. Instead, she scrambled for air, her throat swelling, her muscles spasming.

He loved her.

She loved him.

And . . . she was going to fuck it up. Or he'd realize that he wanted something else, deserved something more. The image of Roxanne burst to life in her mind, and for all she'd worked to exorcise those demons, to embrace her self-worth, to remember that Ethan had pursued her, had showed her over and over again that he chose her . . . she just . . . well, she was just too fucking panicked for something like logic to be effective.

He took a step toward her.

She skittered back. "Stop."

Hurt edged into his expression. "Dani?"

"I can't." A sharp shake of her head. "I just . . . I can't." More time. Space to think. A moment to clear this out, to push back the panic and to come back into herself. Then she could find the words, tell this man—

"You don't love me?"

She shook her head again.

Ethan paled, and she watched in horror as his hand lifted, pressing to his chest, to the spot over his heart, as though the organ inside ached.

Pain splintered through her.

He staggered back.

She stepped forward, realizing that he'd thought the shake was in answer to his question. That wasn't what she'd intended, not at all. She'd just been trying to clear her head. To stop the fucking tornado in her mind.

"Ethan."

He'd been staring at his feet, but the sound of his name on her tongue had him looking up. "It's okay, Dani."

There was a note of resignation in his tone.

One that had the panic in her disappearing in an instant.

As though he'd expected this all along.

"That's not what I meant—"

He turned and disappeared down the hall.

Horror froze her in place for a long moment then she hurried after him. Because fuck the panic, fuck having to think.

She needed to tell Ethan she loved him.

But when she made it out to the bar, it was to find that Ethan and his parents were gone. She spun in a circle, searching, and then caught a flash of him, walking toward the front doors of the hotel.

All but running through the lobby, she snagged his arm just before he would have pushed out.

"Ethan," she began.

Constance turned. "Oh, there you are, honey. Ethan said you'd gone up to bed." She stepped forward, pulled Dani into a hug. "I'm so glad to finally meet you. We'll come out to San Francisco soon."

"I—I'd like that," Dani murmured, her eyes on Ethan.

But he wouldn't look at her, just stared out the large plate glass windows.

Brian swept her into a hug the moment Constance released her. "He gives you any trouble, you just call me, and I'll get him in line."

"He won't," she murmured. "You raised a good man."

Ethan flinched, and she stepped out of Brian's arms, reached out to grab his hand. He backed away, moved to the doors so the sensor picked up his presence and the glass panels slid open.

Brian and Constance waved goodbye and walked out.

When Ethan went to follow, she gripped his elbow. "Wait, I didn't mean—"

"I'm going to walk them to their car." He slipped free. "Wait here."

"O-okay," she whispered.

His eyes searched hers for a long moment, and then he turned and walked out the doors.

She waited.

But he didn't come back.

And when, hours later, she knocked on the door to his room, he didn't answer.

Why, fucking why hadn't she just been able to say she loved him, too?

Twenty-Two

ETHAN

They'd hopped on a plane for an early flight.

Meanwhile, he was a ball of misery.

But he was in the business of pretending he wasn't miserable, dodging Dani at the hotel, arriving at the plane mere seconds before they were supposed to take off, and deliberately choosing a seat far away from her.

All to bask in his misery . . . and his idiocy.

He'd fucked up royally. He'd pushed when he should have been patient, and because of that, he'd gotten an answer that stung like a motherfucker.

Dani liked him.

But she didn't feel the same way about him.

Not yet, anyway.

He yanked out his notebook, spreading out his papers and books next to him, determined to focus on his schoolwork, something he'd been neglecting of late, and hockey.

The team typically traveled to their road destinations right after their game, unless there were more than the usual two down days in between matches. It made for a killer type of red-eye, but it was safer than potentially hitting a delay that might make them late for a game.

Because there was nothing professional athletes hated more than being off their routine.

Arriving the day before a game, sometimes getting in a practice or an optional morning skate in, let them get acclimated to the time zone, the weather, to get enough rest and exercise, and to continue their aforementioned routine.

For Ethan, this included joining in on Brit's killer off-day workout and then spending an hour on the bike and another in either the hotel's hot tub or sauna or the arena's—if they happened to have the facilities for the away team. Not all did, including the one they'd be playing at the day after tomorrow— the final game of the road trip.

Which meant that he'd wake up in the morning, be tortured by Brit and company, and then head back to the hotel for food and hot tub time.

And all the while, he would be pretending that he hadn't fucked up with Dani, that he hadn't blown it, that he wasn't spending all his time trying to figure out a way to explain to her what had gone through his head, and trying to find the strength to not push, to be patient, to hope she'd eventually feel the same way as him—

"Fuck," he whispered, stretching back in his seat, the rumbling of the engines a pleasant drone that would normally make him sleepy. Most of the team was similarly coaxed, the adrenaline wearing down and the familiar sound luring them under. Brit was curled up in a seat across the aisle from him, Coop in the row behind her. If they abided by their routine, Calle would join him shortly, the two lovebirds, still sickeningly infatuated with each other. They'd probably fall asleep holding hands.

Ick.

Also, this just in, he was jealous.

Soft footsteps made him grip his pen tighter, writing faster in the notebook where he was jotting down ideas for one of his final papers. He just wanted to finish it, to get his thoughts on paper, and then he'd try to sleep for a bit.

Try to pretend he wasn't responsible for gouging out his own heart.

The footsteps slowed.

He wrote faster . . . until heat prickled on his nape. Until he glanced up and saw it was Dani.

No, he'd *known* it was her.

That sensation on his skin, the rightness in his chest, the heat arrowing straight for his cock. It was the built-in Dani Locator, and right now she had stopped by his seat. Their gazes collided, and he felt the impact of those gorgeous eyes in his heart, as if she had reached a hand between his ribs and squeezed it tight.

"Hey," he whispered.

Her mouth twitched, as though she'd been going for a smile, but then she seemed to catch herself, nodding and whispering, "Hi." She hesitated. "I . . . about last night. I didn't mean—"

"Say no more," he said. "It's fine."

"It's not fine—"

"Ethan."

They turned, saw that Bernard had come up. "Need a word."

"I—"

With one long look at him, Dani moved back up the aisle. He knew she'd be on her laptop, working until the plane landed, making sure that everything was ready for the team when they needed it. The equipment managers, the trainers, the video coaches—including Dani—were some of the hardest working people in the organization. Their jobs usually began before the players and ended long after them.

The equipment team washed and prepped gear and jerseys for travel, made sure extra sticks, laces, tape, and more were available during the game. They were constantly drying gloves, making sure the players' skates were in good shape, their helmets weren't worn or damaged. Hockey, as a sport, required a shit ton of equipment, and that meant their job didn't stop. But the trainers were just as important. Their job being to keep the players healthy, to come up with workouts and rehab and conditioning plans in order to make sure everyone was skating at their best. Diet was one part. Injury treatment another. Building specific types of muscle strength was still one more. And they had to keep track of that for an entire roster. Not easy.

But as hard as they worked, he'd never seen anyone else pull the kinds of hours Dani did.

Part of the reason he loved and respected her was because she never missed a beat, was always impeccably prepared, a consummate professional. Even as shy as she was with most people, she got her shit done, and the team was the better for it.

In a word, she was amazing.

Multi-faceted. Smart. A hidden well of fire and spine. And pain. And fear. And so much fucking courage.

And he'd fucked up.

He'd pushed her beyond that bravery and into fear, and he'd never forgive himself for doing that. But now, he just needed to figure out how to get beyond that, to convince her to move beyond the scared and trust that he wouldn't hurt her, to believe him when he said he wouldn't push her again. But for all his wants and needs, how could he possibly expect that faith?

"We need to talk about the game tomorrow. I wanted to . . ."

Bernard kept talking, explaining a shift in the system, how he would be playing a bigger role, at least for the time being. Normally, that would have been the best fucking news ever, but today, he was too busy being miserable.

After a few minutes, Bernard moved up the aisle, sitting in his usual spot.

But Ethan's eyes didn't stay on his coach. Instead, they drifted to Dani. Because . . . she was his heart.

"You're staring."

He glanced to the left, away from the aisle that Dani had walked up, saw Fanny leaning against the seat opposite him, her generous mouth curved into a smile. Since she didn't normally fly with them on away games, he asked, "Just couldn't get enough of us?"

The tall, statuesque brunette glanced behind her, then propped herself on the arm of the empty seat next to him. Well, mostly empty since it currently held a stack of his schoolwork.

"Well, actually," she said, lips twitching, "now that you bring it up . . ."

He chuckled quietly. "Visiting family?"

A nod. "Well, I *had* been visiting. We took a road trip of our own, and now I'm with you guys until we fly back to San Francisco. But don't worry, I'll be working plenty. I've got a whole slew of new skating drills to torture you with."

He groaned good-naturedly.

Yes, he hated skating drills. Especially after a lifetime of doing them.

But old—bad—habits crept in quickly, and Fanny kept him straight.

"You love them," she said. Then she leaned in.

Aw, fuck. Here they went.

"Who ya looking at?" she asked casually.

"No one."

"Hmm." A beat. "So, why is Dani walking around with pain and indecision in her eyes?"

He didn't bite.

"Ah, a recalcitrant one." She tapped her chin. "How many ways to destroy your legs shall I use?"

"I fucked up."

"Ah," she said again. "So, I need to destroy you."

He groaned, rested his head in his hands.

She sighed, scooping up his papers and books then sitting down in the seat next to him.

"You know I had a system for that, right?" he muttered.

"I *know* you had a mess." She opened the tray table in front of her, began stacking and organizing the texts in a way that he knew would make sense—just based on her totally organized system of drills both on and off ice, plus keeping track of players' milestones and goals. Fanny was far better suited for balancing a career and degree than he was. "There, now," she said, straightening the stack and turning toward him. "All in order. Now tell me, Dani and you, what's up?"

He made a face. "I told you. I messed up."

"How?" She pointed at said face. "And how badly?"

"Badly." Her expression clouded, and deliberately he dropped his eyes back down to his notebook, ignoring the steady brown gaze trying to force the rest out of him. He'd dealt with Fanny enough on the ice to know that she was a fucking force to be reckoned with once she picked at the thread of something. On the ice for him, it had been his backward crossovers, specifically him not putting weight on the proper edge on his left foot. She'd pulled that out of nowhere, had picked and prodded and drilled the shit out of him until he'd fixed that bad habit. It had taken the entire fucking summer, but he'd managed, thanks to this woman's bulldog tendencies.

And now, she was focused on Dani. On him and Dani.

Things were off. He was moping. Dani was hurt, and Fanny had seen that pain. Which meant it wouldn't be long until the rest of the team would notice.

He'd be getting wooing advice from Kevin, who'd managed to snare PR-Rebecca. Gabe, who was the Gold's head trainer and with Nutritionist Rebecca and really good at asking for forgiveness, would give him a multitude of tips, all while prescribing uncomfortable TENS therapy and/or a pressure point massage as punishment for Ethan's wrongdoings. And Brit would be all over it, enlisting Max and Blue and Coop to enact revenge.

That wasn't even including Blane, Stefan—their former captain and Brit's hubby, Mike, Liam, and Logan.

They'd all have an opinion over his mistakes, would drag him over the coals with one breath, and with the next, they'd want to help him fix his fuck up.

It would be awful.

It would be fucking great.

Because they were family, and they cared.

Ethan just . . . he already had put enough pressure on his own shoulders to try to fix things with Dani. The full-court press of the entire team would probably work against him, make it even harder.

Either that or he was worried that she really didn't love him, wouldn't ever find her way there, and she was just looking for some fun, exploring her attraction to a semi-good-looking guy with a decent job, some smarts, and a nice body. Maybe she didn't actually like what was beneath the surface.

Maybe she didn't see the same future he did.

And perhaps that was the biggest mindfuck of all. Because he wasn't the type of man to back down from what he wanted.

The degree was difficult with his job and travel. He was making it happen. It might have taken longer than planned, but he'd done it. His parents didn't want him to help them when his father had been let go from his job a few years back. He'd paid off their house, refused to accept any repayment when they'd sold it after his parents had both gotten jobs at a different university. He wasn't the most talented guy in the league (not by a long shot). But he'd put his fucking head down and worked to make a place for himself on the special teams. He'd found a way to be valuable and content without trying to be a superstar—not that he had the skill for it.

And that wasn't self-deprecation.

It was reality.

So he was living the fucking dream, feeling fulfilled in his work, in his life . . . well, in most parts of his life.

Because he couldn't make Dani love him. No matter how much he wanted her to.

"Earth to Ethan," Fanny said lightly.

"I'm working," he muttered, squeezing his pen.

"Thinking about Dani. Thinking about how to fix your fuck up."

"Fanny," he warned.

"Ethan," she warned back.

He sighed. "I love her," he said. "But she doesn't love me." His voice dropped to a whisper. "And I can't make her. Even though I really want to."

Fanny's mouth fell open, but he had to give her credit; she recovered quickly. "Ethan, that's—"

"Don't."

"That woman has come alive since you've started dating. She likes you. She *loves* you." Fanny squeezed his hand. "She may not be ready to say it yet, but have no doubt that her heart beats for yours."

The pain in him lessoned, the edges of the gaping wound closing slowly. "I still need to find a way for her to forgive me for pushing."

She snorted. "You're a man. Men push."

"That doesn't make it—" He broke off when her lips twitched. "Hilarious. I should make you do skating drills."

"I'd kill your puny little skating drills." She narrowed her eyes, lips twitching again, and more of that painful, caused-by-his-own-hand wound closed. "Dani is a good person. She's clearly crazy about you. So just be patient but persistent, and"—she leaned in, voice dropping to a whisper—"for the record, she loves Hot Tamales."

"What if she doesn't love *me?*"

Fanny smacked him on the arm. Hard.

The woman was stronger than she appeared, but her tone was even more fierce. "You are a fucking catch, Ethan Korhonen, and if you don't believe that, look inside yourself and imagine how you'd feel if Dani thought that she wasn't worthy of your love."

His jaw clenched as reality struck home.

How could he expect Dani to see herself as he saw her—wonderful, beautiful inside and out, smart, funny, incredibly strong—if he continued to view himself as never quite measuring up?

She nudged him. "Exactly. So put that derision and self-doubt to bed once and for all, woman up, and love her with every bit of your soul."

Fanny was out of the seat and walking down the aisle before he could summon any words, the reality of her words hitting him hard enough to momentarily freeze his lungs.

Because he finally understood.

Self-deprecating took on a different tact when it was laced with self-loathing, when it was used as a joke, but one with a painful center. He stared down at the tray table, knowing that it had begun long ago when he'd overheard one of his father's colleagues telling another colleague that Ethan's parents must be "so disappointed" to not have an "intellectual child."

Because he'd played hockey.

Because he hadn't taken to piano or Math Club. He hadn't had the patience to want to join the debate team.

He loved learning, but only what he found interesting.

Because outside of that, he'd loved even more to *move*—to be on the ice, to feel the cool air on his face, the joy of a teammate scoring or connecting a sweet pass, the terror when a player was streaking back toward their zone, the dip in his stomach when a goal went in their net, the tightness of his lungs, the burn of his quads when he worked his ass off during a shift.

And he'd never quite realized how much how he'd valued that as less.

It had been masked by humor, by self-decrepitation over the years. Yes, the team called him *Big, Juicy Brain*, but he'd never felt that way—and how could he? He knew he was nowhere near as smart as his parents, and he'd been okay with that.

Except . . . he hadn't.

Because beneath all that *okay* was a thorn pressing against the inside of his ribs, jabbing him every time he threatened to breathe too deeply, to look too closely.

For all the joking and pretending to be confident in his place and unaffected by the bullshit that others brought, deep down

Ethan didn't feel like he was enough. When he peeled back the layers, studied what was beneath that veneer, *he didn't feel like enough.* It was a painful fucking truth, because he wanted to be what he appeared to be on the surface, self-assured, comfortable in his space.

He'd found that professionally, felt it like a second skin settling over him by finding his place on the Gold. But as he'd found that, it had masked the rest of the turmoil beneath.

Why his first reaction when Dani hadn't returned his declaration had been to assume that *of course* she couldn't love him back.

Why he'd stayed away, avoided her like hell because he'd *known* that she was going to cut him loose.

Why he'd been so wrapped up in his own head, his own certainty that he wouldn't be enough instead of moving forward with patience and understanding, with openness instead of silent misery.

And, most importantly, finally, *finally* understanding that he could never love Dani properly if he was always worried about being worthy of her heart. He had to believe he was worth it, not to just give her his in an effort to avoid looking beneath.

But *could* he?

As he wrestled with that, with understanding he needed to be able to accept her love so they could build something lasting, his cell—connected to the plane's WiFi—buzzed.

He tugged it from his pocket, saw a text from his mom.

Thanks for letting us crash your date with Dani. She's wonderful.

Yes, she was.

It's not crashing when you're invited. Thanks for coming to the game.

The "..." danced on his screen, and he waited for the message to appear. Waited what felt like an eternity since his mom was a slow texter. But as he did all that waiting, he found his own fingers moving, tapping out a question he didn't really process until it was sent. Until the "..." on his mom's side disappeared.

Do you ever wish you had a different son?

His throat seized, fingers flying again, wanting to explain that he'd meant intellectually, or with a different profession, or—

No.

And then his cell vibrated with an incoming call. From his mom. And fuck, he didn't want to have this conversation, didn't want to delve too deeply, not when the realizations already had him feeling raw.

"Hello?" he murmured, after putting his earpiece in.

"I know you're on the plane," his mom said, her voice an odd blend of fierce and gentle, "so I'll keep this brief. I love you. Just as you are." She paused for a brief moment then went on, "When I see you doing something you love, when I watch you interact with others, demonstrating warmth and kindness and empathy, you make me so fucking proud to be a mother. To be *your* mother. I look at you and feel like my heart is going to explode with pride."

He inhaled, but she kept talking.

"And I'm so sorry that I haven't made that clear, that I made you doubt, that I didn't—" Her voice cracked.

"Mom," he whispered.

She cleared her throat, voice going brisk. "And I know you're on the plane and aren't really supposed to talk on the phone, so I'm going to hang up now. But that doesn't mean that what I just said isn't true." A breath that rattled through the speaker of his earpiece. "And it doesn't mean that I'm not getting on a plane and coming out to San Francisco as soon as possible for us to talk about it in person, okay?"

"Mom," he whispered again.

"Okay?" she repeated.

"Okay," he said.

"I love you."

"I love you, too," he murmured before hanging up and sitting back, his heart pounding, eyes sliding closed. The words washed over him, settling inside, and he felt the wound in his heart start to stitch closed. It wouldn't go away with a few conversations, he knew that. But it was on the way, and he also knew that he'd continue to work on it.

Because he wanted to live without that spike jabbing at him. He wanted to be whole, so he could move forward.

With Dani.

He was *going* to move forward.

With Dani.

Determination washing over him, he glanced up the aisle and saw Fanny staring at him, concern on her face. He nodded, mouthed, "Thanks."

She smiled, nodded, mouthed back, "Family."

Another blip in his heart, more of that wound stitching closed. Because she was family, just as the team was, and he was finally understanding that his place in it was more than professional. It *was* family. Truly. Not just something that was said on the surface or a good sound bite. They saw his value, and he was doing them a disservice to not see the same.

Another understanding came on the heels of that one.

If he kept the team out of this, if he kept their family out of his attempt to win Dani, he'd miss out on *this*. On the family coming together, looking out for one another. He'd miss out on the little insights from some of the people who knew her best, on the advice from his friends who'd won their own happy endings, on the kick in the ass he needed when he was feeling defeated.

This didn't need to be a victory he earned on his own.

He could—and *should*—use every tool in his toolbox.

Flipping the page in his notebook, he began a list.

The first item was Hot Tamales, followed by the types of junk food she'd bought during their grocery shopping outing, during their time together over the last weeks. Luckily, he paid attention to everything that was Dani-related, so within a few minutes, he had a decent list. Or at least, he had enough information to *feed* her.

That was a start.

He spent a few more minutes not working on his term paper as he probably should be doing, but instead making a list of questions to ask Fanny, ideas of things to do to win Dani over, other people he needed to pump for information—Brit, for one, Max, for another (the two biggest gossips around), and Kevin, for a third (because Ethan probably needed to admit that clearly he wasn't the best at romance and again . . . more tools for his toolbox).

By the time he'd filled a couple of pages and his eyes were burning enough that he knew he should give it a rest, he decided that he'd done enough planning for the moment.

He closed the cover, capped his pen, began stacking books, and—

Froze.

Because Fanny hadn't just been organizing.

The woman had deposited a box of Hot Tamales on that tray table, hidden amongst the books like an Easter egg.

Burning eyes forgotten, he ran a finger along the edge, smiled.

And then he pulled out a piece of paper, wrote a note, and tucked both into his bag.

He'd arrange for a special delivery later.

Twenty-Three

Dani

It was an hour until game time, and she was feeling absolutely wretched.

Since that night in Baltimore, since the brief interaction on the plane, she hadn't seen Ethan.

He'd disappeared while she'd waited for her bag.

And when she'd found his room number, had finagled a key by begging, borrowing, and stealing, he hadn't come back to his room, even though she'd slept in his bed and had waited.

She'd bungled things.

Badly.

She needed to make them right.

Only, she didn't know how. And now, she was trying to find a way to make it all right. But how the hell was she supposed to make it all right if she couldn't even lay eyes on the man she loved?

Hell, twenty minutes ago, she'd even gone to the locker room, prepared to announce her love to the entire locker room if need be.

But she'd gotten to the door, found it was locked to everyone outside of the players, and had come back to prep for the game, her wretchedness rising by the second. How was she supposed to focus on her computer when she couldn't tell the blasted man that she was fucking in love with him?

Groaning, she rested her hands on her head, her elbows on her desk.

Knock. Knock.

She dropped her hands, glanced up, and saw Kevin lounging outside the door to the office she'd commandeered. A far cry from her plush space back at the Gold Mine, it nonetheless did the job.

"H-hey, Kev," she managed.

He smiled. "How's it going?"

Her lungs felt tight, small talk with the gorgeous, built man not easy, especially when it felt as though her heart had been pierced straight through. Still, he was one of the biggest teddy bears on the roster, so she got over her shy, her pain, and spun her chair to face him. "I'm good."

Ugh.

She was so *not* good.

"Dani?" Kevin asked, tone concerned.

Double ugh.

Now she was lost in fucking thought instead of focusing on the man in front of her. "Sorry," she said, pushing out of the chair and moving toward the door. "What can I do for you?"

"Nothing."

Her feet skittered to a stop. "Um . . ."

He held up a box. "I think this is for you."

Turquoise paper. A pretty silver bow.

She shook her head. "That can't be."

He turned it in her direction so she could see there was an envelope taped to the top of it, and sure enough, her name was scrawled on the top in large, blocky letters.

"I—" Another shake of her head.

Kevin crossed over to her, pressed the small box into her

hands. It rattled quietly, as though there were lots of small, hard things inside. "Go easy on him," he said, once she'd wrapped her fingers around it. "The man's just starting to learn the art of romance."

"What—"

He winked, was gone a moment later, well before the faltering question made it past her lips.

Dani had been left alone in the quiet room when her watch buzzed. She glanced down to see it was her assistant, Jess, telling her she was ready and waiting for them to complete their pregame check. Jess stayed back in San Francisco on away games, their tag-teaming engulfing both coasts—or in this case, the Midwest and the West Coast.

She voice-texted back, asking for five minutes, able to hear that her tone was off, her words shaky, all because of a tiny, rattling box held in her hands, but beyond glad that the artificial intelligence wouldn't pick up on her anxiety when it transcribed her words.

Technology was her friend.

For the moment, she had five minutes.

Sucking in a breath, staring at the box, debating opening it, she stroked the shiny ribbon for a few moments (which only further served to remind her of her fuck up with Ethan) before curiosity got the better of her and she slipped the bow off then tugged the envelope free. The flap was open a moment later, her fingers pulling out the note inside. As she processed the words, her lips curved up into a smile, and she felt a giggle bubble up, mix with relief in her throat.

Sweetheart,
Wouldn't want your body to get low on all that refined
sugar.
-E

Then she ripped off the paper, her head shaking in disbelief at the contents of the rectangular-shaped box.

Hot Tamales.

Probably the single type of candy she loved that she hadn't actually bought with him on their trip to the grocery store and only because she had already ordered a giant stash, one that filled up nearly an entire shelf in her pantry. A stash she'd bemoaned to Fanny about forgetting to hit up before they'd gone on the road trip—stupid feelings making her forget the important things in life.

Refined sugar.

Cinnamon.

Ethan.

But the appearance of this yumminess meant that Ethan had mind-reading abilities, either that or he'd snooped in her cabinets.

Or . . . Fanny had spilled the contents of her bemoaning on the plane.

There was a knock on the door before she'd delved too deeply into that, into what else Ethan might have learned over the last few days. She swiveled in her chair.

Mandy, one of the team's trainers, stood there, warmth in her eyes and another box in her hands.

"This is for you," she said, crossing the room and setting it on the desk next to Dani. A squeeze of her shoulder, no further words, and Mandy was gone.

More turquoise paper.

Another silver bow.

No note on the outside, but she discovered that was because the note was inside the box, folded and placed in a small silver and turquoise-speckled bowl that had been painted with, "Dani's Candy."

She unfolded it with shaking fingers, read it, and was . . . touched and hopeful and charmed . . .

And still just a bit scared.

Okay, a whole lot scared.

But also, a whole lot relieved. Because Ethan wasn't avoiding her—or she supposed he *was* avoiding her, but he didn't hate her. Rather, he was being sweet and sending her notes, and . . . God, she loved him.

Her fingers trailed over the slanted letters of the note, the crisp handwriting.

For your sugar stash.
-E

She ran a finger around the smooth, glazed edge of the bowl, and then, very carefully, she opened the Hot Tamales and poured in the inch-long red cylinders.

As she suspected, the box filled it perfectly to the top.

"How?" she whispered. "Why?"

But there was no one around to answer her quiet questions, so she spent the next ten minutes on the phone with Jess, going through their checks, making sure all would run as smooth as possible while the game was running.

And during this time, she was interrupted by no less than three more players.

First Max, who handed her a brand-new pair of ridiculously pricey Bluetooth headphones she'd mentioned wanting to Ethan in passing once. Then Coop, who came bearing her favorite coffee. And finally, Blue, a giant smile on his face as he deposited a box that turned out to hold the softest, cuddliest hoodie ever.

Yes, she put it on.

Yes, she drank the coffee while it was hot.

Yes, she synced the headphones with her laptop.

And . . . yes, she fought off the urge to storm the locker room, to grab Ethan and kiss him senseless. Barely.

Knock-knock.

She glanced up, jerking her hand away from the bowl and the smooth edge she kept fondling to see Brit standing in the open doorway in her usual pregame workout gear, worn during her warmup of running through the arena. She also wore a knowing smile and held yet another small package in her hand.

Christ, at this rate, Dani wouldn't have any room in her luggage.

"What now?" she found herself snapping. Then immediately slapping her hand over her mouth. "Sorry," she mumbled, the word muffled. "I . . ."

"Long day?" Brit asked.

She dropped her hand. "You have no idea."

Brit's brown eyes twinkled. "I will neither confirm nor deny any ideas held."

Dani stuck her hand out. "Just give it to me, already. I don't want Ethan's mission to mess up your routine."

"Who said anything about Ethan?"

"*Brit,*" she warned.

The tall blond moved toward her. "I've never seen you growly," she teased. "If it's because of the aforementioned certain yummy, bearded man, then I say it's a good look on you."

"You have your own scruffy, bearded man," Dani muttered, lifting her hand.

One brow went up. "And so I should keep my hands off yours?"

Dani felt her cheeks warm. Thank God, her skin didn't reveal her blush. "I didn't say that."

The second brow joined the first. "It was implied."

"No, it wasn't."

Brit pointed at the monitors. "Should we go to the tape?"

"You're not funny." A beat. "No, go get ready to make all sorts of pretty saves I'm going to chop up into awesome bite-sized replays."

"For the record, I like you with attitude." She squeezed Dani's shoulder, turned away.

"What about the bag?" Dani asked when Brit started to leave with it.

"Who said it was for you?" A teasing question, but before

Dani could start sputtering, embarrassment flooding forward to take hold, Brit plunked the bag down. "Ethan's a good guy," she said. "Love him. It'll be good for you both."

Then she was gone, the door clicking closed behind her.

"I'm trying to love him," Dani muttered, tossing her hands up. "If only the damned man would stop avoiding me."

Twenty-Four

Ethan

"She seemed like she wanted to murder me," Brit said, strolling into the locker room and plunking her ass onto the bench next to him. "I'm assuming you know what you're doing?"

"Mad is better than running screaming for the hills," he replied, picking up his skate and checking his laces, his edges.

Brit paused, head tilting from side to side as she considered that. "Okay, you may be smarter than I anticipated."

He punched her on the shoulder.

Not lightly, because she didn't appreciate her teammates going easy on her. But also not hard, because she was his goalie, and he needed those arms in fighting shape for the game.

She scowled. "*Ow.*"

"Liar."

A beatific smile. "That's true." She clapped her hands together. "What was in my bag?"

He knew what she meant without needing her to clarify. He hadn't told any of his "assistants"—as Kevin had termed them when he'd asked his friend's advice for winning over Dani—what was in the packages, and thankfully they were nosy enough to just be happy about being part of the process, not needing to know every detail.

But Ethan had known that wouldn't last.

And sure enough, Brit had that look. The one that told him she wasn't going to let this drop, not until he gave her the dirty details.

He picked up the other skate, studied the edge, making Brit wait because he thought it was funny as hell that she was impatiently wiggling like a puppy on the bench next to him, curiosity threatening to make her burst.

Just before she got to that point, he set down the skate, turned to her, and said, "A bag."

Her brows formed a little V on her forehead. "That's cheating. I already know I gave her the bag."

He chuckled. "No, Brit. The present was a bag."

Her face screwed up. "Just to confirm, what was inside that cute turquoise bag was, in fact, another bag."

His lips twitched. "Yup."

"A fancy bag?"

He shook his head. "Nope."

More screwing up. "What kind of bag?"

"I don't know." He shrugged out of his shirt, slipped into the skintight one he wore under his gear. "One of those ones with the opening at the top and the straps."

"A tote bag?"

"Yup. That sounds right." He unbuttoned his pants, shoved them down, and pulled on his jock.

"You had me deliver a *tote bag*."

"Yup."

"Just a tote bag?" she asked. "Without gold straps, and it wasn't filled with diamonds or chocolate or anything, right?"

"No gold. No chocolate. No diamonds. Just a bag."

"Brit! Stop snooping, and get your ass in gear!" Max yelled from across the room.

She scowled, jabbed a finger in his direction. "I can't believe everyone else got to deliver cool things, and I gave her a lame tote bag."

"She needed something to hold all the cool things," he pointed out. "And also, the bag had a badger on it."

More V-deepening in her brow. "A badger?"

"Because she's fierce." He smiled, didn't share that it was also because she had a badger tattooed on her foot, just added, "Especially when cornered."

Brit's face smoothed out, shock in her eyes.

Then she nodded approvingly. "Yeah, Eth," she said, punching him on the shoulder, "I am *so* glad I'm helping you with this."

———

The game ended up in a shootout, one they'd lost, much to Brit's consternation.

But the season was long, and they were in the early days yet. They always wanted the two points, but they'd take one, and a game where they'd ultimately played well, followed their system, even though the bounces hadn't gone their way.

That happened sometimes.

The Hockey Gods weren't smiling down at them, or whatever.

Still, they weren't professional athletes because they liked losing. It stung like hell, especially in the close ones, but Ethan, at least, had gotten better at compartmentalizing it away. He'd have tape to watch, a practice or two to try and flush out those mistakes, and then they'd have another game in two night's time.

Play hard. Take the licks. Rework the negative. Highlight the positive.

And do it all over again.

Done.

In the meantime, though, he needed to hope that his parade

of gifts had begun the process of winning Dani over, because he needed to see her, needed to talk to her, needed to fix this . . . with more words and fewer presents.

"Ethan!"

He glanced behind him, stopping on the threshold of the locker room.

Scarlett, PR-Rebecca's assistant, her hair as red as her name, hustled up, clutching an iPad in one hand, using her other to push up her glasses. Her blue eyes shone with worry.

"What's up?" he asked, stepping toward her.

"I fucked up," she whispered, darting a glance over her shoulder. "I am *so* getting fired. This is the first time I've been on my own, and Rebecca finally trusted me to pick up some of her slack, and I am so *totally* going to get fired." She groaned, and he figured she was approximately a millisecond from freaking out.

Which was why he just crouched a little bit, enough to meet her blue eyes, and asked, "What can I do to help?"

"You're late for a meet-and-greet," she hissed. "A meet-and-greet," she added in reply to what was no doubt a confused expression on his face, since he didn't have any fan interactions scheduled. He always received notice before, always had them cleared with him just in case . . . and *ah*, he realized, finally comprehending her miserable expression, *that* was her fuck up.

"You're going to tell Rebecca, aren't you?" she asked dejectedly.

He patted her shoulder. "Let's worry about the fans before we panic about Rebecca," he said. "Give me the specifics."

She rattled them off.

"Okay," he said, stripping off his jersey. "I've got this."

And truthfully, he didn't mind this kind of thing. He wasn't a big draw, so these interactions weren't frequent enough to be draining, and when they involved kids, like tonight's, they were extra special.

"You're definitely going to report me, aren't you?" she asked morosely, as they walked down the hall. "It's my fault. I didn't tell—"

His shoulder pads were driving him crazy, so he took those off next. "If you can get these to Richie"—the equipment manager—"then we'll call it even."

"That's not—"

"It's fine," he said, squeezing her hand. "I promise you, this is fine."

"You'll still tell Rebecca, won't you?"

Ethan paused, considered that. "I'll have to if she asks," he said truthfully. "But I don't see why she'd specifically ask about this. She'll ask if you did your job well. She'll want to know that you care about the team as much as she does." He squeezed her shoulder. "And my answer to both of those will be yes."

Relief slid through her expression.

"You good with the gear?" he asked, less because he needed her to take care of his shoulder pads and more because he felt like she needed something to do that wasn't worrying about stepping into PR-Rebecca's shoes.

"I'm good," she whispered.

"Thanks," he said, handing them to her, and then he moved toward the teeny, tiny little girl and her mom, crouching down to talk about his three favorite things: hockey, more hockey, and . . . YouTubers.

Grinning over the girl's—Catherine's—head, he saw her mom sigh and open her mouth, like she was going to interrupt, but he shook his head, letting her know it was all good, and then listened as Catherine explained what sounded like a very intense trick shot that had been performed by her favorite, yup, he'd guessed it, YouTuber. "Do you think you could do it?" she asked once she'd finished.

He solemnly shook his head. "No way."

Her face fell.

"But I bet you'll be able to do it before I can."

She smiled wide enough to light up the already bright hall then threw her arms around his neck. "You really think so?"

He nodded. "I know so. Also," he said, handing her the jersey he'd stripped off earlier. "This is for you."

Another huge smile that had his heart squeezing tight. "Really?"

"Really."

Catherine yanked it over her head, practically swimming in the fabric, but she was happy, her mom was happy, and he chatted with them for a few more minutes. It got harder to concentrate as those minutes passed because he felt *it*.

Or rather *her*.

As Catherine spoke, his nerves prickled, the skin on his nape prickled, awareness filling every cell. His inner Dani detector was on full alert, telling him she was near.

He wanted to break off the conversation, to track her down.

But he wouldn't.

Because this moment was one of the big ones, an important interaction, something that—even at risk of him sounding egotistical—but it might be something Catherine remembered forever.

So, he'd give the little girl his time, his patience.

His complete focus.

Also, this just in, apparently men *could* multitask—or at least his inner Dani detector could still work while he listened to Catherine chatter. He felt her watching him, sensed her staying in place.

And that gave him the strength to finish the conversation.

Eventually, though, Catherine yawned, and her mom bustled her away after he'd signed the jersey, thanking him. He scored one more hug and a super special fist bump before mom and daughter disappeared down the hall, Scarlett swooping in out of somewhere to show them the way.

Thankfully, that inner detector was still blazing strong.

He turned, his gaze immediately arrowing in on Dani.

Twenty-Five

"Why do you like to be called Fanny?" she asked her friend, who was lingering in her office waiting for the bus to the airport and the plane that would take them home.

"What's going on between you and Ethan?" Fanny countered, making Dani's mouth drop open and her finger slip as she nearly deleted the wrong video file. Quickly, she closed and saved everything, knowing she could finish the rest of her work on the plane, when she wasn't at risk of crashing her whole system.

"Nothing," she squeaked.

"Sure." Plump lips turned up. "You were all lovely-dovey for a few weeks, and now I'm surrounded by mopey Joes, but nothing is going on." She sank onto the edge of the desk. "Also, I go by Fanny because every other girl in school growing up was named Stephanie." A shrug. "Being Fanny helped me stand out from the fold. Plus, I had plenty of opportunities to practice my comebacks for someone comparing me to a butt and/or a vagina."

Dani shuddered. "That sounds horrible," she said.

"Life is horrible sometimes." Another shrug. "You might as well control the shitty parts as much as you're able."

"That's actually kind of deep."

"I can be deep," Fanny said. "Just like I know that you're in love with the man, and yet you're not in his arms making goo-goo eyes at him."

Dani groaned, covered her face with her hands. "I blew it," she said. "He announced he loved me, and I freaked out. Yes, I love him, too. I've loved him for ages, but by the time I found the words, he was all shut down, and now I keep trying to talk to him, but he's either hiding or avoiding me and . . ." She groaned again, banged her head on the table, and wailed, "I still haven't been able to tell him that I love him!"

"He can't avoid you forever," Fanny said, "you work together."

"Well, he's done a damned good job of it so far," she muttered, opening her laptop.

"It'll be okay," Fanny said.

"How?" Dani lifted her head. "I hurt him."

Fanny squeezed her shoulder. "He loves you, babe. *That's* how I know it'll be okay. Plus, you have this organization of perfectly matched soul mates to serve as an example of how everything will work out." Another squeeze. "It's almost sickening how many HEAs we have among the Gold. You two are in good company."

"I know, but . . ." Dani sighed, cut herself off, hating that even though she had so much love for Ethan, she was still worried it might all implode.

Fanny bumped her shoulder. "Self-reflection builds character, but too much can freeze you in quicksand." Brown eyes gentling. "There is always risk in life, always a chance it might go wrong. But courage goes to those who can grab on to their happy." A flash of a smile, before her face went serious. "Because when you love someone, when you stop being afraid and just go for it then . . ." She released a breath. "It's like that, as simple as breathing, but you finally feel like your lungs can work fully. You can be yourself without fear, without being so locked down that you're not open to new experiences. You can be . . . happy."

Dani ran her thumb lightly back and forth along the space bar on her laptop, not hard enough to depress the key, just enough to feel the warmed plastic slide along her skin. "You make it sound easy."

Fanny pressed her thumb down on the key. "It is easy. As easy as striking a key," she said, returning her hand to her lap, "and it's also the hardest thing you'll ever do."

"Is that what your experience was like with love?"

Fanny smiled sadly. "That's a story for another time, preferably when I've had an entire pitcher of daiquiris."

"I'm sorry, Fan." Her eyes went to the single space on the blank document, the cursor blinking to its right. "I'm sorry you were hurt."

"I'm not." She swallowed. "Now, I have it on good authority that a certain sexy, bearded forward is . . ." She named a location that wasn't too far away.

No fear.

Just rightness.

"Excuse me," Dani said, pushing up out of her chair and moving to the door. "I need to go to him . . ."

"Dani?" Fanny called just as her fingers wrapped around the cool metal of the doorknob.

She stopped.

"For the record, no one is allowed to tell you how to feel. Not even me and my pushy self," Fanny said with a smile. "And definitely not those asshole inner voices. Just . . . throw in some mental earplugs and listen to your heart. That will always give you the strength to make the right decision." Fanny went to the door, warm brown eyes staring into hers, turned the knob, and opened it wide. "You got this." A wink. "Plus, love and the power of the Gold are on your side."

Dani released a long, slow breath and nodded.

Fanny smiled approvingly. "It's just that easy, babe." A beat. "Now, go on and tell that man what he means to you."

Dani slipped into the hall, moving toward the place Fanny had mentioned, knowing there were a million other post-game things she *should* be doing, and number one of those was that she shouldn't be walking out of the office she used while at this arena. She should be labeling and splicing and loading content onto devices, emailing it out to players and coaches so they had it before they could even think about wanting it. But tonight, as she took that first step, as she strode down the hall and passed the tunnel that led to the arena, the cool air of the ice hitting her skin, she paused and watched the men and women walk across the rink, repairing it, prepping it for the next game.

And she found peace . . . and courage.

Ethan could run, but she'd find him.

He could avoid her, but she wouldn't stop showing Ethan she loved him.

So, yes, there was courage inside her.

Instead of pain and fear, anxiety and insecurity. Those sharp spikes that had lived inside her for so long, eased by Ethan but still hiding in the background, threatening, waiting, making it so she had to breathe carefully and move cautiously, lest she do either wrong and jab herself . . . they'd retreated, disappearing into the ether.

Permanently.

Because she loved Ethan.

She turned away from the rink, and with that simple thought on her mind, in a sort of perfect moment of symmetry, she spotted Ethan.

Dani watched as he, still in the bottom half of his gear, his strong chest and arms on display with a tight black undershirt, smiled and fist-bumped a little girl who was maybe seven, the Gold jersey she wore engulfing her from her neck nearly down to her toes. After they spoke for a few minutes, he gently reached for the little one, those hands giant on tiny shoulders as he spun her so he could use the marker her mom held out to sign his name.

That done, he handed the pen back, and they talked for a little while longer. But he didn't seem to be in any rush, even though he had to be tired, had to be wanting a shower and to get out of that wet gear.

Finally, he took some pictures, got a hug and another fist-bump, and waved at the mother and daughter as they disappeared down the hall.

Dani waited, hardly breathing, and the moment the daughter and her mom were gone, Ethan turned, his eyes coming unerringly to hers, as though it wouldn't have mattered if she possessed the ability to camouflage with her surroundings, he would have still known she was there.

Her lips parted on a silent exhale, her heart thumping against her ribs.

He walked toward her.

Clunk. Clunk. Clunk.

Then he was there, towering over her even more than normal with the extra inches gained from his skates, and her nose was filled with the scent of salt and spice and . . . Ethan.

"I'm sorry," she blurted.

His eyes gentled. "Sweetheart," he murmured, his hand wrapping around her wrist in one smooth move—as though it were an unconscious action, as though he'd greeted her that way for an eternity, with his slightly roughened fingertips running along the delicate skin there. "I'm the one who's sorry. I shouldn't have rushed you. I should have—"

Unbidden, her eyes burned, her throat working as she attempted to swallow the sob bubbling up in its depths.

She wanted this.

She wanted *him*.

"I love you, Ethan."

"Sweetheart," he said gently, his thumb drifting a little higher.

"I've been trying to find you all damned day, wanting to tell you that from the moment you left with your parents." She grabbed his shoulders, shook him lightly. "I was surprised, yes," she murmured. "And scared. And had a full-on panic attack." She inhaled sharply, released it slowly. "Truthfully, I am still a little scared because what I feel for you is so big, so intense, so much more than I'd ever hoped. But I love you, so fucking much."

Her eyes continued to burn, and in a heartbeat, she lost her battle with tears, one sliding down her cheek, a hot, liquid brand, then more streaking in their wake. "I thought I'd messed it up." She sniffed. "I thought I'd lost you, and for one second, I wanted to give up." She shook her head. "But I won't give you up, even if you keep trying to avoid me and push me away."

"I wasn't."

She blinked at the fierceness in his tone. "What?"

"I wasn't trying to push you away," he said, cupping her jaw. "I fucked up. I hurt you. I *scared* you. I needed to find a way to prove to you that I would wait." He rested his forehead to hers. "I needed to make it up to you. To—"

She yanked out of his hold.

"You stupid, stubborn man!"

His mouth fell open.

"That was a universally stupid thing to do!" she snapped, shoving away from him.

"You didn't like the gifts?"

She froze, spun back. "They were wonderful."

"So, why am I stupid?"

"Because you could have come back, and we could have talked it out, and I didn't need the gifts. I was miserable and hurt, and I —I just needed you."

A warm chest pressed to her back, arms around her middle. "You're right. It would have been much simpler to talk. Though I wouldn't have gotten the whole team on my side, helping, wouldn't have learned you loved Hot Tamales. Wouldn't have gotten to shower you with the small gifts that are only a fraction of what you deserve."

"I didn't need—"

He spun her to face him. "But I did. I needed to give them to you, and I'm going to keep giving you everything you need in a thousand different ways."

"Eth—"

"I love you. I'm going to take care of you."

"I feel the same—"

His thumb brushed over her lips.

"But I didn't think I deserved you. I had this well inside me that said because I'm not as smart as my parents because I'm not the most talented player on the ice, that because . . . so many other things . . . I thought you couldn't want me. That I'd need to be more." His hand slid down, lightly gripped the side of her neck. "And for you, I *want* to be more."

"I don't want more. I just want *you*."

He shuddered, his chin resting on top of her head, his arms banding tight, drawing her against his chest. Probably, she should be disgusted to be wrapped in the sweaty embrace of a man who'd just spent the last three-plus hours working his ass off, but instead of that, she was just wrapped in everything that was this man—his scent, spice and salt, but not unappealing; his gentle touch, his arms slipping around her, holding her carefully; and his words, softly whispered in her ear, words of love and romance, ones she didn't fully process at first, except to understand that the tone was smooth and easy, and then she did, and more tears joined those on her cheek, her lungs breathing.

Because this man was wonderful.

Ethan ran his hand up and down her back, calming her, still murmuring gentle words, comforting her without telling her to stop crying.

Because she hated that, hated when someone told her to not cry.

And of course, he instinctively knew that, just continued to whisper that he "had her," and held her tight, stroked her gently until she'd gotten herself under control, until the tears no longer came, and the sobs quieted.

"Sorry," she whispered, wiping her eyes and cheek with the hem of her shirt, glad that what little makeup she wore was waterproof and so wouldn't end up with her fun, sparkling gold eye shadow smeared all over her face. "This was supposed to be a romantic moment, but now I snotted all over you."

"You never need to apologize for letting me hold you," he said, cupping her cheek, thumb drifting up and wiping away some moisture she had missed. "Snot or otherwise."

Inhaling and exhaling slowly, Dani shook her head. "I didn't mean to lose it. I—"

"Dani."

She was already forming the next reply in her mind, started to pull herself out of his arms. "I just. It's been a lot and I—"

His hand on her waist tightened, holding her against him. The one on her cheek stayed gentle. "Dani."

"And I—"

"*Dani*," he said. "I'm telling you this in the nicest possible way." A beat as she watched laughter trickle into his expression, his mouth softening, so fucking tempting that she wanted to rise on tiptoe and close the distance between their lips. "But please, just shut the fuck up."

Outrage down her spine.

A gasp of indignation on her tongue.

But he didn't stop talking, just continued to hold her stare as he said, "I love you." That thumb swept forward, traced over her bottom lip. "You've held my heart in your palm from the moment I first saw you stroke an iPad, from the second you laughed and let those amber eyes meet mine."

She wrinkled her nose. "They're just boring brown."

"Lies." He shook his head, hand sliding up, thumb now lightly drifting across the bottoms of her lashes. It tickled, but she didn't back away. "You have tones of mahogany and amber in there, tiny streaks of gold and russet. I swear," he said, tone going a little husky, "every single time that you let me see them, I find a different shade in them."

Her pulse skipped around in her veins, as though someone had somehow dumped Pop Rocks into them. "I like your eyes, too," she whispered.

He smiled, that lovely turn up of his lips Dani felt in the depths of her soul—sticky cotton candy on her fingertips, sweetness tingling on her tongue, warmth in her belly . . . desire pooling between her thighs.

"Dani?" he asked again, and God, she loved the way he said her name.

"Yeah?" she whispered.

"I'm going to kiss you now." A millisecond later, his mouth was on hers, his palm tilting her head back so their lips were perfectly aligned, his hand on her hip drawing her a little closer, until she could feel his shin guards pressing against her legs, the thick protective hockey pants he wore firm against her pelvis and stomach, his chest hard where it met hers, his muscles gloriously clad in just that thin, black material. Her nipples tightened, her womb clenching in her abdomen, her pussy growing damp.

His tongue flicked against her mouth, deftly parting her lips to drift inside her mouth, to tangle with hers.

She rose on tiptoe, drifting closer, her tongue and lips not shy but joining in the glorious dance with him. The world fell away. She forgot about his gear, about the cool air of the ice drifting down the tunnel—she was plenty warm in his arms anyway. She forgot all about the publicness of their position.

And she wouldn't care anyway.

Because the team was part of their love story.

And anyway, Ethan was the only thing she could process.

His body, hard. His touch, gentle. His ability to melt the very marrow of her bones, vast.

His kiss, marking the beginning of their happy ending.

His hand slipped from her cheek to skate along her jaw, to drift up into her hair, fingers tangling in the curls, and he kept his mouth on hers, kissing her until she was a bundled ball of nerves, *desperate* for more.

He nipped her bottom lip, kissed her deeper, hauled her closer.

She moaned, nipped him back, and murmured, "I love you."

He froze and for one instant, the kiss got somehow even hotter. Their bodies coming even closer together, her hands gripping his shoulders, his drifting down to cup her ass, but then as things were just getting *really* good . . .

He pulled back.

With a wince.

Horror and embarrassment flooded through her. Oh God, she'd . . . done something. Hurt him somehow. Shit. He'd taken a puck to the ribs during the game.

She must have hit it.

She jumped back, flinching when his fingers caught on her hair for a heartbeat. "I'm so sorry," she said, fumbling with the words, her hands wringing in front of her as she stood in that cool tunnel.

Ethan took her hands. "You're sorry for giving me the hottest kiss of my life? For returning my love? For making me the happiest I've ever been?"

Well, put it that way.

She was sucked into the thunderstorm of his eyes. "I'm sorry I hurt you."

"I love you, you ridiculous woman." He straightened, a slow breath slipping out of his lips. "But what could possibly make you think I was hurting?"

"I saw you wince."

Now a smile teased the edges of his mouth. "I don't suppose you noticed that I'm still half-dressed."

Dani blinked at the humor of his tone. "Um, yes, I *did* notice that."

"Well"—hint of pink tinged his cheeks—"there's not really a delicate way to say this except to confide in you that an erection in a cup isn't exactly conducive to comfort . . . or blood flow."

Formal words that took her a moment to process.

Then when they did . . . her mouth dropped open, and her gaze . . . well, it dropped south, arrowing in on the region covered by hockey pants and the aforementioned cup. "You're hard right now?"

He groaned, put a finger under her chin, tilting it back up. "Not helping, sweetheart," he murmured. "I've got to go back into that locker room, and I can't be swinging my hard dick around."

"But I like seeing you swing it around. I especially liked it when you—"

"Not cool, Dani," he murmured, pressing a kiss to her mouth, though his eyes sparked with humor. "I'm trying to not have a boner, and you're not helping my problem."

"I like your—"

"You're a menace," he growled.

A blip of pride wove through her.

No one had ever called her that before. "I love you."

"God." His breath whispered against her mouth. "I love it when you smile like that."

"Like what?"

"Heat on the edges, sweet in the center." He groaned again. "One more, and then I promise I'll shower before I take you back to the hotel room and show you how good I can swing my cock around."

"We're hopping on the plane after this."

"Fuck." A pause, dancing storm cloud eyes on hers. "Mile high club?"

She burst out laughing. "I can barely fit into the bathroom, let alone both of us."

A grin, a brush of his thumb. "I think we can do anything we put our minds to."

She nipped that thumb. "Even loving a stubborn, shy woman?"

"*Especially* loving a shy, stubborn, wonderful woman," he said. "Now, give me my one more."

Before she could agree to that sentiment—and for the record, she would have wholeheartedly agreed—but before she could tell him yes, before she could just flat out kiss him again, his lips were on hers, his tongue in her mouth. Both hands went to her ass, lifting her against him, narrowing the distance so he didn't have to bend so far, their height difference dramatic with him in his skates.

And . . . then she stopped thinking about the movements and height difference and slipped back into strictly feeling, soaking into the sensations his kisses evoked. The prickles of his beard on her skin, the slight tickle of it brushing along the underside of her nose. Desire licking along the underside of her skin, burning along the edges of her nerves.

"Fuck," he gasped, breaking away so quickly that she wobbled on her feet, might very well have toppled over if not for him catching her shoulders and righting her.

"Yes," she murmured.

He smiled. "Yes, what?"

"Yes, we can try for the Mile High Club."

Ethan burst out laughing, bending at the waist, coaxing laughter out of her until her cheeks hurt.

Until that happy ending was a living, breathing thing within her.

He tugged one of her unruly curls, smiled that special smile just for her. "You just try and get rid of me."

Her breath caught, and she almost launched herself right back into his arms, the temptation to taste him, to hold on to this lovely, buoyant, confident feeling so strong that she didn't want to chance not feeling it again.

But then Brit came around the corner, Fanny at her shoulder, and both women took in Dani's closeness to Ethan, his hand still on her shoulder, both of them flushed, their lips kiss swollen. In an instant, Brit grinned and clapped her hands together. Fanny smiled, nodding approvingly.

And knowing this was going to be fodder for the gossip train —and not giving a damn—she found herself turning toward Ethan, tugging his head down, and kissing him with every bit of joy and love she felt.

Then she pulled away, loving the red staining his cheeks, the dazed look in his eyes. His fingers were tight on her hips, his lips glistening from their kiss. She nudged him back, stepped away. "I'll see you on the plane."

And then she walked past Brit, knowing she was wearing a cat-ate-the-canary grin, and not giving a damn.

"He's mine," she announced, patting the goalie's shoulder. "My bearded, sexy man."

"Hear, hear," Brit said.

There was no reason to deny it, not when it was in her heart, her soul, not when there weren't any secrets with the team, with her *family*.

Her love for Ethan was forever.

Epilogue
Part One

Ethan, Six Months Later

He was being stared down by three gorgeous women with amber and russet eyes.

"What makes you think that you could possibly be good enough for my Dani?"

"I'm not," he admitted, picking up his glass of water and wishing that when he'd met Dani's mom and sisters, it hadn't been on a night when he needed to stick with the diet plan.

Because fuck, what he wouldn't give for a beer.

"Mama, *stop*," Dani said, sweeping into the room with a big platter of food. She set it on the coffee table then came over to perch on the arm of Ethan's chair. "I love Ethan, and he loves me, so stop doing the whole scary parent thing."

He covered her knee. "I don't think she's *doing* the scary parent thing. I think she *embodies* the whole parent thing."

Dani sighed.

Belle, her mother, smiled. Barely, just the corners of her lips turning up. "You'll do, Ethan. I think you'll just do." He relaxed marginally, and the smile flattened. "For now."

Dani sighed again. "Loni, can you please talk some sense into Mom?"

"Nope." She reached for the platter of cheese and bread and started scarfing both down in rapid succession. "Mom gets to be Scary Mom for all first boyfriend interactions." Loni glanced at him, winked. "But don't worry, she calms down after a while."

Toni was in the midst of filling another plate, though she passed it to her mother, then did the same for Dani and Ethan.

It contained all sorts of things he couldn't eat, but he smiled his thanks anyway.

"For the record, my mother never calms down," Toni said, once she'd made up her own plate.

Dani sighed for a third time.

He chuckled.

She swatted him. "Don't encourage them."

Setting their plates on the table, he tugged her off the arm of the chair, brought her close. "They remind me of you." He kissed the tip of her nose. "So, I'll always encourage them." A beat. "And you." Grabbing her plate again, he held it for her. "Now eat," he ordered.

"Ethan."

He lifted the plate. "Food."

"I'm not."

"*Food.*"

"I'm—"

"Will you just eat the fucking piece of cheese?" Loni burst out.

"Language!" Belle scolded.

But Ethan didn't give a shit about language. He'd gotten fed up with the orders and the plate *and* the cheese. He swapped their positions, dropped her into the chair, and knelt at her feet, tossing the aforementioned cheese onto the table.

That was when she finally noticed it, her eyes going wide, her mouth parting on a gasp. "Is that—?"

That being the diamond ring Toni had done him a solid by hiding.

"Dani," he murmured. "I love you"—he glanced behind him—"and your family—"

"You haven't met my dad yet—"

"He has, baby," Belle said. "He's met all of us. And Daddy approves."

Dani sucked in a breath, her eyes wide.

"I—" He froze, all the pretty words he'd had planned in his brain drifting off into nothing, leaving him with a fuzzy tongue and a desperation to hear this woman say yes. "I love you—"

"You said that already," Loni grumbled.

"Shh!" Toni whisper yelled.

Dani lifted a brow. "You seriously volunteered to include them in this?"

"They're your family," he said. "Our family, and I want us to —want *you* to have everything you've ever dreamed of."

"I have you," she murmured. "Which means I already have it."

Fuck, he loved her.

"Dani Eastbrooke, will you—"

"Yes, she will!" Loni burst in. "Now kiss her already so we can have more cheese."

"Loni Eastbrook, you will be the death of me," Belle began.

"God, seriously, I wonder if you were adopted," Toni muttered. "You're ruining a perfectly happy and romantic—"

Ethan tuned them out. "Will you marry me, sweetheart?"

She slipped out of the chair, knelt with him. "You sure you want to be part of that mess?" A nod over his shoulder, where the voices were rising in volume.

"I can't wait to be part of that mess."

Tears leaked out of the corners of her eyes. "Then, yes, baby. Yes, I'll marry you."

Then with a conversation—no, an argument about the proper merits of really good cheese happening in the background, the voices increasing in volume, he slid the ring on her fourth finger.

And then he kissed her to the sound of a debate over ranch vs. blue cheese.

A glimpse of his happy ending.

And a damned perfect one at that.

————

FANNY

She glanced down at the text from Dani, the picture of the gleaming diamond ring on her finger, and smiled.

Yeah, Dani was one of the good ones, and she deserved the good that Ethan brought into her life.

She typed out an enthusiastic response then set her cell on the counter and blinked rapidly. She'd had that once. The diamond ring, the loving fiancé, the wonderful, joyous hope of a future.

But it had all been taken away.

As she'd tried on wedding dresses.

"Fate can be a real bitch sometimes," she muttered, going to the cabinet and retrieving a glass—a big glass—because she was most definitely happy for her friend, because she wasn't the kind of woman who wanted everyone else to be miserable just because her happy ending hadn't worked out.

Shit happened.

Unfortunately, a heap of that shit of life had landed on her shoulders.

She opened the fridge, pulled out the stopper on her bottle of wine, and then poured a generous splash into her glass.

And then remembering the diamond ring that had once sat on her own finger, she poured another long splash.

"Come on, Fan," she murmured. "You're going to change into pajamas, put on a face mask, and watch the *Saw* franchise until you forget all about failed romances and remember that you have a very fulfilling life."

She paused, considered that.

Then nodded once, proud of her very sound plan.

Bringing her wine with her, since it was the first step of necessary oblivion, she made her way upstairs and into her bedroom, slipping into pajamas even though it was barely five in the evening.

"Plan, Douglas," she muttered. "Stick with the plan."

Right.

Wine. Check. Pajamas. Check. Mask. Next on the agenda.

She reached for the very expensive jar, washed her face, smeared on the cream, and then she belted on her robe, grabbed her glass, and headed back downstairs, plugging a food order into her cell for the fattiest, greasiest carb load she could find.

In forty-five minutes, she was going to be at a great place.

Nearing a heart attack.

But all the happier for it.

"Movie," she whispered, cueing it up as she popped some popcorn—because if she was going for greasy and fatty, she needed that, too.

Pretty soon, she was on the couch, the slasher flick rolling, buttery fingers gripping her wine and feeling so much better for it. There was no thought of unhappy endings, no heartbreak and pain.

Just actors on a screen playing a part.

And a nice buzz floating through her brain.

She wouldn't think about the past, about Brandon—

The doorbell rang, just in the nick of time.

She paused the movie before jumping up and hurrying down the hall, her memories chasing her like the hounds of hell. The food was early, thankfully, would take her mind further off everything that had happened.

Flicking the lock, she turned the handle, pulled open the door, expecting to see a delivery person with a bag in hand.

Instead, she saw . . .

She blinked.

Impossible.

The wine had gone to her head, because he could not be on her porch. She was hallucinating. The alcohol content of the pinot noir was higher than she'd expected. This was food, that was all—

"Brandon?" she whispered.

The figment of her imagination stepped forward, the shadows disappearing from his face.

"It's me, Fan."

Her lips parted, every cell inside her waiting for his next words.

"I remember," he murmured. "I remember *everything*."

Her buttery fingers spasmed, and she lost her hold on her wine.

Glass shattered.

Red splattered all over her bare feet.

"Oh, no," she whispered, her breath catching. "Not again."

———

Thank you for reading! I hope you loved meeting Dani and Ethan! The next book in the Gold Hockey series is CRASHED.
Once upon a time she'd had the happy ending.
Then *everything* had been taken from her.

CLICK HERE TO READ CRASHED NOW>.

And if you enjoyed Caged, you'll love the sexy, sweet, and close-knit Breakers Hockey crew. <u>The first book in the series,</u> <u>BROKEN, is now live!</u>

Her life was a disaster...Don't miss the hilarious Life Sucks series, starting with TRAIN WRECK. Derek Cashette was determined to salvage the train wreck of her life...and she was just as determined *not* to let him be the hero.

DOWNLOAD TRAIN WRECK FOR FREE at www.elisefaber.com/train-wreck

I so appreciate your help in spreading the word about my books, including sharing with friends! Please leave a review on your favorite book site!
You can also join my Facebook group, the Fabinators, for exclusive giveaways and sneak peeks of future books.

SIGN UP FOR ELISE FABER'S NEWSLETTER HERE: https://www.elisefaber.com/newsletter

————

Want a free bonus story? Hate missing Elise's new releases? Love contests, exclusive excerpts and giveaways?
Then signup for Elise's newsletter here!
https://www.elisefaber.com/newsletter

————

And join Elise's fan group, the Fabinators https://www.facebook.com/groups/fabinators for insider information, sneak peaks at new releases, and fun freebies! Hope to see you there!

GOLD HOCKEY SERIES

Gold Hockey (all stand alone)
Blocked
Backhand
Boarding
Benched
Breakaway
Breakout
Checked
Coasting
Centered
Charging
Caged
Crashed
A Gold Christmas
Cycled
Caught
Cap

Gold Hockey

Did you miss any of the Gold Hockey books?
Find information about the full series here.
Or keep reading for a sneak peek into each of the books below!

Blocked
Gold Hockey Book #1
Get your copy at https://www.elisefaber.com/blocked

Brit

The first question Brit always got when people found out she played ice hockey was *"Do you have all of your teeth?"*

The second was *"Do you, you know, look at the guys in the locker room?"*

The first she could deal with easily—flash a smile of her full set of chompers, no gaps in sight. The second was more problematic. Especially since it was typically accompanied by a smug smile or a coy wink.

Of course she looked. *Everybody* looked once. Everyone snuck a glance, made a judgment that was quickly filed away and shoved deep down into the recesses of their mind.

And she meant *way* down.

Because, dammit, she was there to play hockey, not assess her teammates' six packs. If she wanted to get her man candy fix, she could just go on social media. There were shirtless guys for days filling her feed.

But that wasn't the answer the media wanted.

Who cared about locker room dynamics? Who gave a damn whether or not she, as a typical heterosexual woman, found her fellow players attractive?

Yet for some inane reason, it *did* matter to people.

Brit wasn't stupid. The press wanted a story. A scandal. They were desperate for her to fall for one of her teammates—or better yet the captain from their rival team—and have an affair that was worthy of a romantic comedy.

She'd just gotten very good at keeping her love life—as nonexistent as it was—to herself, gotten very good at not reacting in any perceptible way to the insinuations.

So when the reporter asked her the same set of questions for the thousandth time in her twenty-six years, she grinned—showing off those teeth—and commented with a sweetly innocent "Could've sworn you were going to ask me about the coed showers." She waited for the room-at-large to laugh then said, "Next question, please."

–Get your copy at https://www.elisefaber.com/blocked

Backhand

Gold Hockey Book #2

Get your copy at https://www.elisefaber.com/backhand

SARA

"Sorry I messed up your sketch," he rumbled.

She nibbled on the side of her mouth, biting back a smile. "Sorry I stole your hand for so long."

He shrugged. "My mom's an artist. I get it."

Well, there went her battle with the smile. Her lips twitched and her teeth came out of hiding. If there was one thing that Sara had, it was her smile. It had been her trademark in her competition days.

Which were long over.

Her mouth flattened out, the grin slipping away. Time to go, time to forget, to move on, to rebuild. "Thanks," she said and extended a hand.

Then winced and dropped it when her ribs cried out in protest.

"You okay?" he asked, head tilting, eyes studying her.

"Fine." And out popped her new smile. The fake one. Careful of her aching side, she shrugged into her backpack. "I've got to go." She turned, ponytail flapping through the hair to land on her opposite shoulder.

"That—" He touched her arm. "Wait. I *know* I know you."

She froze. That was the second time he'd said that, and now they were getting into dangerous territory. Recognition meant . . . no. She couldn't.

There had been a time when *everyone* had known her. Her face on Wheaties boxes, her smile promoting toothpaste and credit cards alike.

That wasn't her life any longer.

"Thanks again. Bye." She started to hurry away.

"Wait." A hand dropped on to her shoulder, thwarting her escape, and she hissed in pain.

"Sorry," he said, but he didn't release her. Instead, he shifted his grip from her aching shoulder down to her elbow and when she didn't protest, he exerted gentle pressure until Sara was facing him again. "It's just that know I *know* you."

No. This wasn't happening.

"You're Sara Jetty."

Her body went tense.

Oh God. This was *so* happening.

"It's me." He touched his chest like she didn't know he was talking about himself, and even as she was finally recognizing the color of his eyes, the familiar curve of his lips and line of his jaw, he said the worst thing ever, "Mike Stewart."

Oh *shit*.

—Get your copy at https://www.elisefaber.com/backhand

Boarding

Gold Hockey Book #3

Get your copy at https://www.elisefaber.com/boarding

MANDY

Hockey players had the *best* asses.

No pancake bottoms, these men—and *women*—could fill out a pair of jeans. She wanted to squeeze it, to nibble it, bounce a dime—

Mandy dropped her chin to her chest, losing sight of the Sorting Hat cupcakes she'd been pondering.

Blane with his yummy ass had a unique way of distracting her.

No, it wasn't even distraction, per se. He had *always* been able to get under her skin.

And that was very, very bad for her.

"Ugh," she said, tossing her phone onto her desk and standing, knowing that she wouldn't be able to sit still now.

Nope, she needed about forty laps in the pool and a good hard fu—

Run, her mind blurted, almost yelling at the mental voice of her inner devil. *A good hard run.*

Unfortunately, the cajoling tone wasn't completely drowned out. *Some sexy horizontal time with Blane would be more fun—*

But the rest of the enticing words were lost as the roar of the crowd suddenly penetrated through the layers of concrete. Her stomach twisted. Mandy could tell, even before her eyes made it to the television, that it wasn't in celebration of a goal or a good hit either.

This was fury, a collective of outrage.

She was on her feet the moment she saw the prone form lying so still face down on the ice.

Her gut twisted when she spotted the curving line of a numeral two on the back of the player's jersey.

"Not him," she said and the words were familiar, a sentiment she had whispered, had *prayed* a thousand times before. She needed the camera angle to shift, for her to be able to see more clearly *who* was hurt. "Not him."

Then Dr. Carter was on the ice and the player moved slightly, rolling away from the camera, giving a full shot of his back and the matching twos adorning his jersey.

Fuck. Not him. Not Blane.

And that was when she saw the pool of blood.

—Get your copy at https://www.elisefaber.com/boarding

Benched

Gold Hockey Book #4

Get your copy at https://www.elisefaber.com/benched

MAX

He started up the car, listening and chiming in at the right places as Brayden talked all things video game.

But his mind was unfortunately stuck on the fact that women were not to be trusted.

He snorted. Brit—the Gold's goalie and the first female in the NHL—and Mandy—the team's head trainer—would smack him around for that sentiment, so he silently amended it to: *most* women were not to be trusted.

There. Better, see?

Somehow, he didn't think they'd see.

He parked in the school's lot, walked Brayden in, and received the appropriate amount of scorn from the secretary for being thirty minutes late to school, then bent to hug Brayden.

"I'll pick you up today," he said.

Brayden smiled and hugged him tightly. Then he whispered something in his ear that hit Max harder than a two-by-four to the temple.

"If you got me a new mom, we wouldn't be late for school."

"Wh-what?" Max stammered.

"Please, Dad? Can you?"

And with that mind fuck of an ask, Brayden gave him one more squeeze and pushed through the door to the playground, calling, "Love you!" over his shoulder.

Then he was gone, and Max was standing in the office of his son's school struggling to comprehend if he had actually just heard what he'd heard.

A new mom?

Fuck his life.

—Get your copy at https://www.elisefaber.com/benched

Breakaway
Gold Hockey Book #5
Get your copy at https://www.elisefaber.com/breakaway

BLUE

"Thanks for the ride."

"Try not to go out and get a fresh bimbo to ride tonight. I hear STIs on are the rise in the city."

Blue sighed, turned back to face her. "Really?"

She shrugged, smirk teasing the edges of her mouth, drawing his focus to the lushness of her lips. "Just watching out for Max's teammate."

He rolled his eyes. "Not hardly."

"Okay, how about I'm trying to prevent you from spreading STIs to the female populace."

"I'm clean, and I'm smart," he told her. "Condoms all the way."

"Ew."

Except there was something about the way she said it that made Blue stiffen and take notice. Because . . . he stared into her eyes, watched as the pale blue darkened to royal, saw her lips part, and her suck in a breath.

Holy shit.

"You're attracted to me."

Her jaw dropped. "No fucking way," she said, too quickly, pink dancing on the edges of her cheekbones. "You're delusional."

Blue got close.

Real close.

Anna licked her lips.

And fuck it all, he kissed that luscious mouth.

—Breakaway, https://www.elisefaber.com/breakaway

Breakout
Gold Hockey Book #6
Get your copy at https://www.elisefaber.com/breakout

PR–Rebecca

A fucking perfect hockey fairy tale.

Shaking her head, because she knew firsthand that fairy tales didn't exist outside of rom-coms and occasionally between alpha sports heroes and their chosen mates, Rebecca slipped through the corridor and stepped onto the Gold's bench.

Lots of dudes in suits—of both the boardroom *and* the hockey variety—were hugging.

On the ice. Near the goals. On the bench.

It was a proverbial hug-fest.

And she was the cynical bitch who couldn't enjoy the fact

that the team she was with had just won the biggest hockey prize of them all.

"I knew you'd be like this."

Rebecca turned her focus from Brit, who was skating with the huge silver cup, to the man—no, to the *boy* because no matter how pretty and yummy he was, Kevin was still a decade younger than her—leaning oh so casually against the boards.

"Nice goal," she told him.

A shrug. "Blue made a nice pass."

And dammit, the fact that he wasn't an arrogant son of a bitch made her like him more.

She nodded at the cup. "You should go have your turn."

"I'll get mine," he said with another shrug.

She frowned, honestly confused. "You don't want—"

Suddenly he was in front of her on the bench, towering over her even though she was wearing her four-inch power heels. "You know what I want?"

Rebecca couldn't speak. Her breath had whooshed out of her in the presence of all that sweaty, hockey god-ness. Fuck he was pretty and gorgeous and . . . so fucking masculine that her thighs actually clenched together.

She wanted to climb him like a stripper pole.

"Do you?" he asked again when her words wouldn't come. "Want to know what I want?"

She nodded.

He bent, lips to her ear. "You, babe," he whispered. "I. Want. You."

Then he straightened and jumped back onto the ice, leaving her gaping after him like she had less than two brain cells in her skull.

The worst part?

She wanted him, too.

Had wanted him since the moment she'd laid eyes on the sexy as sin hockey god.

"Trouble," she murmured. "I'm in *so* much fucking trouble."

—Breakout, https://www.elisefaber.com/breakout

Checked

Gold Hockey Book #7
Get your copy at https://www.elisefaber.com/checked

"Rebecca."

She kept walking.

She might work with Gabe, but she sure as heck wasn't on speaking terms with him. He'd dismissed her work, ignored her contribution to the team. He'd made her feel small and unimportant and—

She kept walking.

"*Rebecca.*"

Not happening. Her car was in sight, thank fuck. She beeped the locks, reached for the handle.

He caught her arm.

"Baby—"

"I am *not* your baby, and you don't get to touch me." She ripped herself free, started muttering as she reached for the handle of her car again. "You don't even like me."

He stepped close, real close. Not touching her, not pushing the boundary she'd set, and yet he still got really freaking close. Her breath caught, her chin lifted, her pulse picked up. "That. Is. Where. You're. Wrong."

She froze.

"What?"

His mouth dropped to her ear, still not touching, but near enough that she could feel his hot breath.

"I like you, Rebecca. Too fucking much."

Then he turned and strode away.

—Checked, https://www.elisefaber.com/checked

Coasting
Gold Hockey Book #8
Get your copy at https://www.elisefaber.com/coasting

Coop

Without thinking, he caught her arm.

"You're not okay."

She shuddered to a stop when he touched her, not fighting the grip, chin dropping to her chest. "No," she said, "you're right. I'm not okay."

"Who was on the phone?" he asked gently.

Her jaw went tight. "My ex."

Fury blazed through him. "Did he hurt you?" he growled.

A shake of her head. "Not like you're thinking." She sucked in a breath. "He broke my heart."

Coop's own heart gave a twinge. "I'm sorry, Calle. That's—"

"Fucking stupid." Another tear joined the first, dripping down the pale skin of her cheek.

"It's not stupid to have loved someone," he said gently.

Her eyes went fierce. "It's incredibly stupid when the person who supposedly loves you right back doesn't give a damn that you're pregnant."

His jaw fell open. He knew it did.

But Calle? Even, gentle *Calle* had gotten knocked up and—

"Yup," she said, brushing by him. "See? Really *fucking* stupid."

And without another word, she disappeared into the rink.

—Coasting, https://www.elisefaber.com/coasting

Centered
Gold Hockey Book #9
Get your copy at https://www.elisefaber.com/centered

"Watch out!"

The warning came a second too late.

He'd already stepped off the curb, already put himself in range of the car that was blowing through the red light, tearing through the intersection, not giving a shit that there were pedestrians walking—

Well, of all the ways to go, at least this would be quick.

But just as the car came within an inch of him, Liam found himself jerked back onto the curb, his one-hundred-and-eighty-pound frame becoming unwieldy and clumsy.

Kind of like on the ice over the last few years.

That was his last thought before he found himself sprawled, ass first, on the San Franciscan sidewalk.

Gross.

"What. The. *Fuck?*" a female voice snapped.

The same female voice that had warned him.

"Do you have a fucking death wish?" she yelled, causing his eyes to snap open, making him look up at an angel . . . a foot tapping, arms crossed, seriously pissed, and seemingly way too small to have been able to haul his ass back onto the curb female.

Liam thought he just might have that death wish.

Especially if it meant he got to be rescued by a woman who looked like an angel. He opened his mouth to reply.

But apparently didn't work fast enough.

Because the woman, the beautiful, curvy female, made a disgusted noise and strode away from him.

He watched her go, watched that gorgeous ass stride down the sidewalk, and stop outside a storefront.

And suddenly, he thought that, hockey or not, he might just want to stay in San Francisco after all.

—Centered, https://www.elisefaber.com/centered

Charging
Gold Hockey Book #10

Get your copy at https://www.elisefaber.com/charging

"Your feet hurt."

Her brows drew together. "What?"

Logan nodded at her feet, clad in a lovely pair of heels that, while beautiful, were also the equivalent of bear traps—and if that wasn't the perfect metaphor for the man in front of her, she didn't know what was.

"Those heels hurt you." His head tilted to the side. "Why do you wear them?"

She scoffed. "None of your fucking business, Walker."

A smile—slow and hot and sliding like silk over her breasts, her stomach, between her legs. "I knew you'd say that."

"I—"

He held up a box she hadn't noticed, pushed it into her hands when she stepped back. "Open it," he said, voice dropping and joining that silk of his smile to dip between her legs. "If you think you can handle it."

And then he was gone, the door closing behind him, leaving her with a heavy ass bag packed with who knew what, aching feet, and a box in her hands.

A box given on a challenge.

A box he knew she'd open.

Because Charlotte Harris didn't give in or back down. She liked that even less than she liked losing.

So, she opened the lid.

And instantly knew she was in trouble.

—Charging, https://www.elisefaber.com/charging

Checked

Coasting

Centered

Charging

Caged

Crashed

A Gold Christmas

Cycled

Caught

Cap

Breakers Hockey (all stand alone)

<u>Broken</u>

<u>Boldly</u>

<u>Breathless</u>

<u>Ballsy</u>

<u>Bewitched</u>

Love, Action, Camera (all stand alone)

Dotted Line

Action Shot

Close-Up

End Scene

Meet Cute

Love After Midnight **(all stand alone)**

Rum And Notes

Virgin Daiquiri

On The Rocks

Sex On The Seats

Life Sucks Series (all stand alone)

Train Wreck

Hot Mess

Dumpster Fire

Clusterf*@k

FUBAR (March 29,2022)

Roosevelt Ranch Series (all stand alone, series complete)

Disaster at Roosevelt Ranch

Heartbreak at Roosevelt Ranch

Collision at Roosevelt Ranch

Regret at Roosevelt Ranch

Desire at Roosevelt Ranch

Phoenix Series (read in order)

Phoenix Rising

Dark Phoenix

Phoenix Freed

Phoenix: Lex Tal Chronicles (rereleasing soon, stand alone, Phoenix world)

From Ashes

In Flames

To Smoke

KTS Series

Riding The Edge

Crossing The Line

Leveling The Field

Scorching The Earth

About the Author

USA Today bestselling author, Elise Faber, loves chocolate, Star Wars, Harry Potter, and hockey (the order depending on the day and how well her team -- the Sharks! -- are playing). She and her husband also play as much hockey as they can squeeze into their schedules, so much so that their typical date night is spent on the ice. Elise changes her hair color more often than some people change their socks, loves sparkly things, and is the mom to two exuberant boys. She lives in Northern California. Connect with her in her Facebook group, the Fabinators or find more information about her books at www.elisefaber.com.

facebook.com/elisefaberauthor

amazon.com/author/elisefaber

bookbub.com/profile/elise-faber

instagram.com/elisefaber

goodreads.com/elisefaber

pinterest.com/elisefaberwrite